Legend of the Paymaster's Gold

Legend of the Paymaster's Gold

Jo Shawyer

DUNDURN
TORONTO

Editor: Nicole Chaplin
Design: Jesse Hooper
Printer: Webcom

Library and Archives Canada Cataloguing in Publication

Shawyer, Jo
Legend of the paymaster's gold / Jo Shawyer.

Issued also in electronic formats.
ISBN 978-1-55488-990-7

I. Title.

PS8637.H392L45 2012 jC813'.6 C2011-902590-6

1 2 3 4 5 16 15 14 13 12

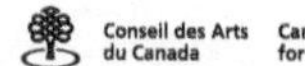

Canada

We acknowledge the support of the **Canada Council for the Arts** and the **Ontario Arts Council** for our publishing program. We also acknowledge the financial support of the **Government of Canada** through the **Canada Book Fund** and **Livres Canada Books**, and the **Government of Ontario** through the **Ontario Book Publishing Tax Credit** and the **Ontario Media Development Corporation**.

Care has been taken to trace the ownership of copyright material used in this book. The author and the publisher welcome any information enabling them to rectify any references or credits in subsequent editions.

J. Kirk Howard, President

Printed and bound in Canada.
www.dundurn.com

Dundurn	Gazelle Book Services Limited	Dundurn
3 Church Street, Suite 500	White Cross Mills	2250 Military Road
Toronto, Ontario, Canada	High Town, Lancaster, England	Tonawanda, NY
M5E 1M2	LA1 4XS	U.S.A. 14150

For Bruce, my partner in my literary adventures!

Legend: noun — traditional story popularly regarded as historical, myth.

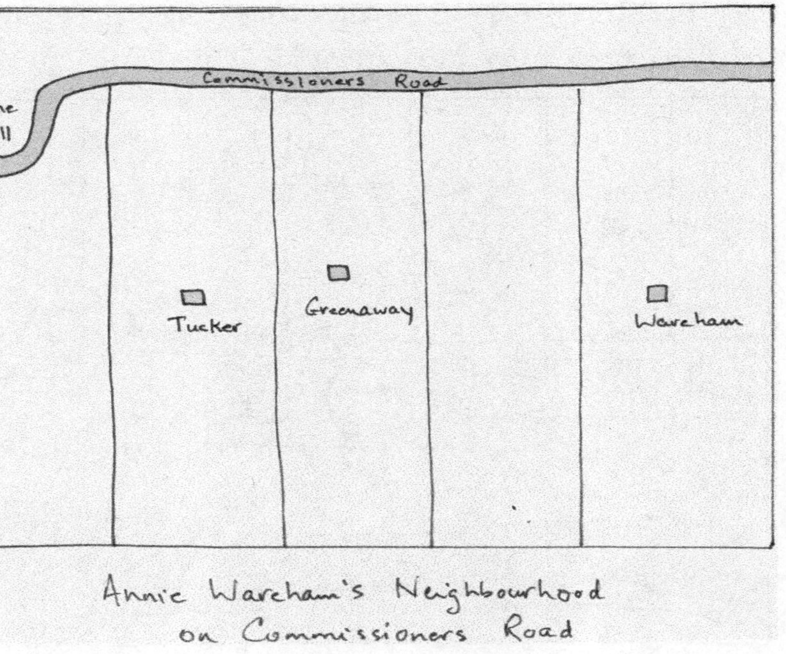
The Hill
Commissioners Road
Tucker
Greenaway
Wareham
Annie Wareham's Neighbourhood
on Commissioners Road

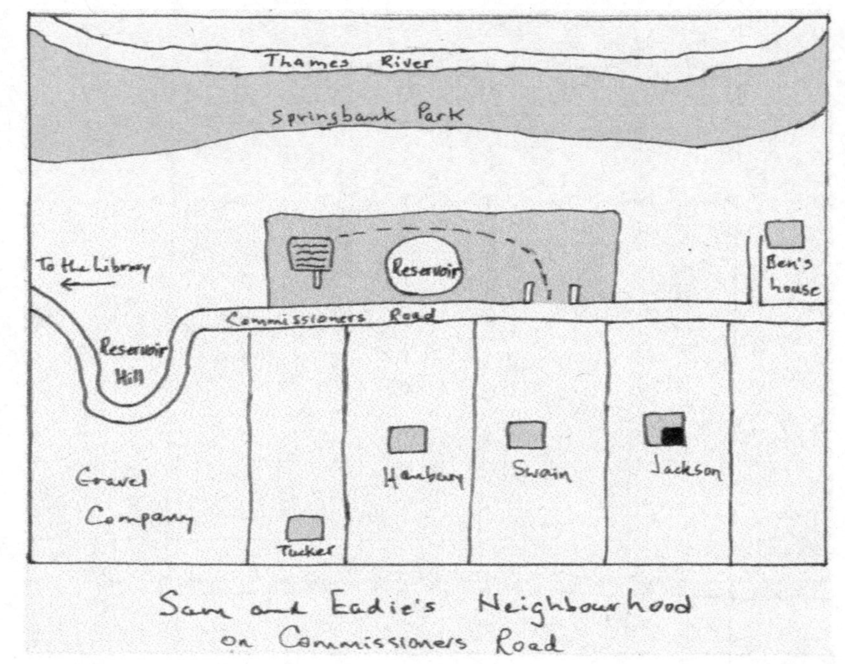

Sam and Eadie's Neighbourhood on Commissioners Road

Chapter One

Annie Wareham, Her Journal

June 1811

Finally we are here at our new place. It's my birthday! I am thirteen years old today. We walked all the way from the New York country to this new frontier in Upper Canada. Daisy and Bessie, our cows, walked all the way, too. Father and John, my older brother, and Cousin Ned are making us a shelter for the summer. But I like sleeping under the stars better. Cousin Ned shot a deer today. Mother and I spent all day smoking the meat. We smell like smoke! Father is glad that this land is on Commissioner's Road. He says that farms and towns will develop quickly nearby. I hope so. I want to make some new friends. Father and Mother are pleased to be here in a British colony. And so is John. But Cousin Ned who came with us to help us settle wishes that we had never left New York. Some Indians came by today and gave us some fish.

"It's weird. This house is really weird." Eadie stood in the empty kitchen of the empty house, and looked around carefully. "From the outside, the house is square, but inside it's not. There's a whole chunk missing." She turned to look at her twin brother, Sam, and her parents, Tom and Liz Jackson. "How can that be?"

This was Sam and Eadie's first visit to their new home. It was an old house on an old road at the edge of London, Ontario. They were moving in the next day. The house seemed odd right from the start.

Tom agreed. "It is strange, Eadie. Your mum and I thought so, too, when we first came to look at this place. The room at the back corner of the house has no door connecting it with the rest of the house, not even to the kitchen. So, you can only enter from outside the house. I think it's always been used as a shed."

"It seems pretty dumb to me," grumbled Sam. "Why build a house and not connect all of the rooms?"

Tom and Liz looked at each other and sighed. They were all feeling grumpy. They had loved their old house downtown and were still coming to terms with the fact that the city had expropriated it to widen the street. Forced to move, Tom and Liz had chosen this house at the edge of the city, close to the countryside, on a big piece of land, where they would have no risk of being expropriated again.

They liked that it was an old house. Mrs. Foster, who had sold them the house, told them that it was built in 1865. And Commissioners Road was built very early in pioneer times. The Jacksons also liked the fact that the house was on the top of a hill, Reservoir Hill, with Reservoir Park across the road.

From this house, it would be easy for their parents to commute to their jobs in the city. But it was harder for Sam and Eadie. They would have to change schools and leave their friends behind. It looked like a long, boring summer ahead.

"I want to break down the wall between that shed-room and the kitchen," Liz said. "That will make it part of the house. It could be a dining room or a sunroom."

"Let's have a look." Tom led the way through the kitchen and out the back door. Sam followed. At fourteen he was almost as tall as his father, but a lot thinner and with more hair — dark curly hair that tumbled in all directions.

Eadie followed behind. She was tiny like her mother, and, like Sam, enjoyed sports. But even more, she liked to be curled up with a book, alone. She liked to write stories and always had a notebook handy to jot down ideas. Although she didn't like moving house and having to change schools, she was at least glad that they had moved from one old house to another old house. *Old houses have seen a lot of history. This house should have some stories to tell,* she thought as she trailed along after Sam and her dad.

Liz followed Eadie out the kitchen to the back of the house and then to the door leading into the shed-room. Short and energetic, she was determined that her family learn to like this house and the neighbourhood.

Tom wrestled with the rusty old key and shouldered open the door to the shed-room. They peered inside. Having no windows, the room was dark. They pushed the door wide open to let some light in, and saw that it was full of junk. There was a big chair with its stuffing falling out, a table with one leg missing, paint cans, a couple of filthy carpets, some empty cardboard boxes, and many pieces of lumber. The walls were roughly plastered and very grimy. There were mouse droppings everywhere.

"Gross," Eadie said.

"Double gross," Sam said.

Liz sighed. "This will need clearing out. More work." She glanced at Sam and Eadie. "But not today."

"Let's check out the park," Sam suggested.

Sam and Eadie left their parents to discuss renovations to the house. The twins crossed the road to the elaborate gate at the entrance to Reservoir Park. The gate was made of iron bars and hung on two sturdy stone gateposts. On each gatepost there was a sign.

"What's all this about?" muttered Sam.

The sign on the gatepost on the right was dated 1920. It described the construction of the reservoir, which Sam and Eadie could see in the distance. It was a huge, circular, cement-covered area surrounded by a high embankment. Sam shrugged. "What a dumb park. It's just a water reservoir where they collect water for the city. Are we supposed to get excited about the fact that it can hold ..." he peered again at the plaque, "'ten-million imperial gallons of water'?"

"That was in 1920, Sam. Look at this other sign. The first reservoir was built in 1878. That's more than 100 years ago."

"A historical water supply." Sam shook his head. "Heritage, I guess."

"At least the park is free," Eadie said as they entered through the gate. They followed the track around the edge of the reservoir when, suddenly, the track narrowed and they entered a thick woods. It was dark and silent.

Eadie looked up at the tall trees where their branches met overhead. "This is more like a forest than a woods, Sam. Look how big around the trunks of the trees are. They must have been growing here since pioneer times."

"Maybe they've been here since the first reservoir was built. Anyway, it's awfully gloomy."

The path led to a wooden shelter with open sides and a roof shaped like a mushroom. Here they could see that they were up very high, looking out over the valley of the Thames River below. But they couldn't see the river itself because the large trees blocked the view.

Eadie spied a historical plaque beside the wooden shelter. "Sam, look at this."

"THE WAR OF 1812"

On August 30, 1814, on this section of Commissioner's Road, a company of Middlesex Militia, led by Captain Daniel Rapelje, ambushed a party of some 70 mounted United States Rangers, guided by former Delaware resident, Andrew Westbrook. The Americans were returning to Amherstburg after a raid on Oxford Township (Ingersoll), where they had taken several prisoners, including 4 officers from the Oxford Militia. Such burn, destroy, and abduction raids were the enemy's military strategy for this part of Upper Canada throughout 1814.

Captain Rapelje became aware of the American presence in the area, and in anticipation, constructed a barricade across the ravine-like section of road. The ensuing ambush routed the Rangers, who fled eastward, leaving casualties on the field. All the prisoners escaped except Captain John Carroll of the Oxford Militia, who was killed.

Funded in partnership with the London Advisory Committee on Heritage and the Save the Reservoir Hill Group

Now Sam was all attention. "Cool!" He punched the air with his fist. "A war! A battle! It says right here, The War of 1812. An ambush on this section of Commissioners Road!"

"And someone was even killed! Poor Captain Carroll." Eadie shivered.

"This was a battlefield, Eadie. Right here, on Reservoir Hill." Sam read the plaque carefully again. "Seventy Americans. That's a big raiding party."

"I can't believe it, Sam. I always thought that the Canadians were friends with the Americans."

"Not in the War of 1812, they weren't," a voice behind them said.

Sam and Eadie spun around. There, facing them, was a boy about their age. Short, very skinny. Red hair and a mass of freckles.

He grinned. "Hi. I'm Ben. You must be the new people in Mrs. Foster's place."

Chapter Two

July 1811

Today is hot. Aunt Jessie gave me this book when we said goodbye to her in New York. She told me to practise writing in it because she knew that there would be no school here on this frontier. But there is never time to write in it. We found some grassy patches and dug them up to plant some potatoes and some wheat. We have to walk a distance to them. In between, it is all trees — huge trees — but Father and John and Cousin Ned are cutting them down to make us a small cabin for the winter. We will make a shelter for Daisy and Bessie, too.

A man came today from west of here and told us there is talk of war between these British colonies and America. It is something to do with a war between England and France. I don't understand. Mother is very upset. We came from America to this British Colony. It would be terrible to find that we are at war with where we came from. We have relatives in America — Cousin Ned's parents, Aunt Jessie, and Uncle William. "It is just men, wanting to fight," Mother says.

Sam and Eadie stared at Ben.

"I'm Sam."

"I'm Eadie. Where do you live?"

"Just over there, across the park, on the other side of the reservoir."

Sam got straight to the point. "So … what do you know about the War of 1812? Was there really a battle here? Right here? Is it true?"

"Of course, it's true. There were two battles here. Well, not really big battles with thousands of soldiers, but skirmishes — fights really, but with guns — between small groups of soldiers. One was this ambush," Ben waved a hand at the historic plaque, "and the other was a skirmish involving General Procter. But there's no plaque for that one."

"I thought the War of 1812 was only at Niagara," Eadie said. She was thinking of a school trip that she had been on there. And Forts that they had visited.

"It was everywhere: Nova Scotia, Quebec, and here. You'll hear more about it at school. You can't get through school around here without it," Ben grinned. "War of 1812–1814. It lasted two years. Between us and America."

"Why isn't there a plaque for the Procter skirmish?" Sam asked.

"Because nobody knows whether it really happened. It's a legend." Ben paused for effect. "It's called the Legend of the Paymaster's Gold."

"This is getting better and better," Sam exclaimed. "What's the legend? What's a paymaster? Whose gold was it?"

There, standing in the park, by the plaque, Ben explained. "This plaque is about American raiders who came here in 1814 to harass the settlers. The local militia ambushed them and chased them off." He turned back to Sam and Eadie. "That really happened and Captain Carroll really did get killed."

"But what about General Procter?" Sam was impatient.

"The Legend of the Paymaster's Gold is about General Henry Procter. That happened earlier in the war, in 1813. Procter was retreating from fighting the Americans at Detroit. He followed east along the Thames River, chased by the Americans. They caught up with him and they fought west of here, at Moraviantown, and Procter was totally beaten. He lost hundreds of men and Native allies. The famous Native leader, Tecumseh, died in that battle. That's true, that battle really happened."

"What happened next?"

Ben continued, clearly enjoying himself. "Procter beat it. With the few men who were left. They came along Commissioners Road, right past here, and the Americans caught up with them again right on Reservoir Hill. There was a skirmish. Captain Carroll fought off the Americans while Procter escaped and headed east toward Lake Ontario. And, somehow, some gold went missing. The story is that it was Procter's paymaster who lost the gold. He was in charge of buying food for the men and horses so he must have been carrying a lot of money."

"And nobody's ever found the gold?" Eadie asked.

"No. Because it's only a legend. No one has ever proved that the skirmish on Reservoir Hill ever happened. It's just a story."

"So that's why there's no plaque for Procter?" Eadie asked.

"Right."

"I can't stand it!" Sam flung his arms in the air. "Either there was a skirmish on Reservoir Hill or there wasn't. What's the problem?"

"The problem is that no one wrote anything down about it at the time. There's no official report. No document to prove it."

"It's just a story that people have told?"

"Right. It's just a story. A legend."

"Bummer," said Sam.

They stood on the path. Silent. Lost in thought. Then Eadie tucked her long black hair behind her ear and crossed her arms. She grinned at the boys. "But maybe they're wrong. And maybe the legend is true. Maybe the gold really was lost." She paused, and added quietly, "But then, of course, there wouldn't be a legend."

"But then there would be gold!" Sam and Ben grinned at each other.

"Exactly," said Eadie. "And nobody's ever found it, so it must still be lost." She looked around at the path, at the field where the reservoir was, and toward the edge of Reservoir Hill. "Somewhere. Here."

Sam turned to Ben. "Let's search for the gold! What we need is a metal detector."

To Sam's astonishment, Ben replied, "My dad's got one."

"Cool! Have you ever found anything?"

"Not any gold. But we found some musket balls. And some soldiers' uniform buttons."

"This is getting better and better! Can we see them?"

"Sure. They're at my place."

Sam and Eadie followed Ben along the path through the woods to come out on the other side of the giant reservoir. They climbed over a fence and crossed a field to his house. It was more modern than Sam and Eadie's house, but it, too, was set apart from other houses. Ben introduced them to his mother, Mrs. Matthews. She had flaming red hair, too. She was an artist and had a studio in their house. This intrigued Eadie who liked to draw and paint. But today she was more interested in musket balls and military buttons.

Eadie followed Sam and Ben outside to the garage. Ben hauled a large box down from a shelf. "Here's everything I've found. You find more junk than good stuff." In the box were beer bottle caps, a can opener, a ring or two, some rusty nails, and some odd bits of metal. He lifted out a smaller box and opened it. Inside were six musket balls. As big as a large marble, dark and dull-coloured, their rounded surfaces a little irregular. Eadie picked one up. It was surprisingly heavy.

"It's made of lead," Ben explained. "These were shot from muskets. Dad and I looked on the Web and they're definitely from the War of 1812."

"Historically accurate?"

"Absolutely. The musket was called the 'Brown Bess.' The soldier could load and fire three or four shots a minute."

Sam rolled a couple of musket balls in his hand. "I wonder how many a soldier carried. They're heavy."

"So was the musket. It was almost five feet long and weighed about nine pounds."

"How far could it shoot?"

"About 100 yards at most. It was only accurate up to about 75 yards."

Sam thought for a moment. "So, accurate to centre field in baseball? That's not very far, really, if someone is pointing a musket straight at you...."

"Or," Eadie, a tennis player, added, "accurate to the length of three tennis courts."

"Where'd you find the musket balls?" Sam asked.

"They were in all different places. We didn't find them all together."

"But did you find them in Reservoir Park or near Commissioners Road?" Eadie asked.

"Yeah. We found them in these fields at the top of the hill, on this side of the reservoir. My dad says that it's useless to look on the actual hillside because of the depth of the leaf mould and the gravitational slumpage of the soil down the hill."

Sam and Eadie stared at Ben.

Ben grinned. "Yeah, well, that's how my dad talks. He's a biologist."

Sam and Eadie laughed.

Ben opened another little box. There were three buttons. Small, dark, and battered. "They're pewter. That's a mixture of tin and lead."

"Didn't the officers have fancy ones?"

"Maybe. But this is all we found."

Eadie rubbed one of the buttons with her finger. "I wonder what happened to the soldier who lost these buttons?"

"I'm more interested in gold than buttons," Sam said.

"But, Sam, the buttons and the musket balls are proof that there really was a skirmish here, even if no one wrote it down. Maybe the legend is not a legend at all." She looked at the boys. "I think that Procter's paymaster really did lose the gold."

Sam looked at Eadie and Ben. "I vote we search for the gold. When we find the gold, we'll split it even, three ways."

Sam, Eadie, and Ben looked at each other and nodded.

"Fair enough?" Sam said.

"Done." Ben agreed.

They sealed the deal with high fives.

Ben's mother came into the garage, car keys in her hand. "Look," she said, turning to Sam and Eadie. "If you want to know more about the War of 1812 here on Commissioners Road, go to the library. They've got loads of material. But right now, we've got to go to the dentist."

Ben made a face. "See you soon, guys."

Chapter Three

March 1812

Now that spring is here there is talk of war again. It is hard enough to get through the winter months without having to worry about fighting a war in the summer. We have new neighbours called Thomas and William Greenaway. Two old bachelor brothers. They have oxen and that will be a great help to all of us.

Father says that the government wants more families to move to this area. If Britain settles it, then America cannot claim it. The Greenaways will have to build their cabin like the government says, just as we did: 20 feet by 16 feet and 100 feet back from the road. We will help them, like Mr. Tucker and Mr. McNames helped us. I have made a friend with Lucy Tucker along the road. We made maple sugar with the Tuckers. It tastes so good!

"I'm starving," Sam said as he watched the Matthews' car drive away. They followed it down the lane and crossed Commissioners Road to their house.

Talking to Ben had gotten both Eadie and Sam to think a little differently about Commissioners Road. They kept looking around and across the field toward Reservoir Hill. It gave them a funny feeling to think that people had lived in this area for two hundred years. And even watched a skirmish — maybe two — on the hill. It was exciting, but kind of creepy, too.

Liz was laying out a picnic lunch outside on the kitchen step. Sam and Eadie joined her and told both their parents about Ben and what Ben had told them about the Legend of the Paymaster's Gold. They also told them about the two skirmishes on their road, but that only one had been recorded on the plaque. The other one was only a story handed down. A legend. That's why there was no plaque about it.

Liz unwrapped a package of sandwiches — ham and pickle, Eadie's favourite — and thought a moment. "It all makes sense. Commissioners Road was built in the early 1800s precisely for the defence of Upper Canada, so that our troops could get to the Detroit frontier. And it would have been the only road through here in 1812. It would have been used by soldiers, settlers, Natives, enemy raiders from America — everyone."

Eadie waved her sandwich in the air. "It's amazing!" She could easily imagine the soldiers marching by their house two hundred years ago. She could see their scarlet jackets and tall, black shako hats, every soldier hung about with leather straps and pouches to carry ammunition.

Tom put down his sandwich, balanced a tomato on top of it, and rummaged in his shirt pocket for a pencil. He tore a bit of paper from the wrapping in the picnic basket.

He was a city planner, someone who drew maps of the city and planned how and where it was to grow.

"Look," he said, as he sketched southern Ontario on the scrap of paper. He talked as he drew the map. "The war was fought between British Colonies and the United States. We live in what was called Upper Canada. Here is Niagara, the eastern border between Upper Canada and America. Here, to the west, is Detroit, another border between Upper Canada and America. And here is the Thames River. In 1812, from Detroit, you could take a boat across Lake St. Clair, and then come east up the Thames River to the Longwoods Road, and then Commissioners Road, and come right past our doorstep on your way to Niagara. Commissioners Road was the super highway of the War of 1812!"

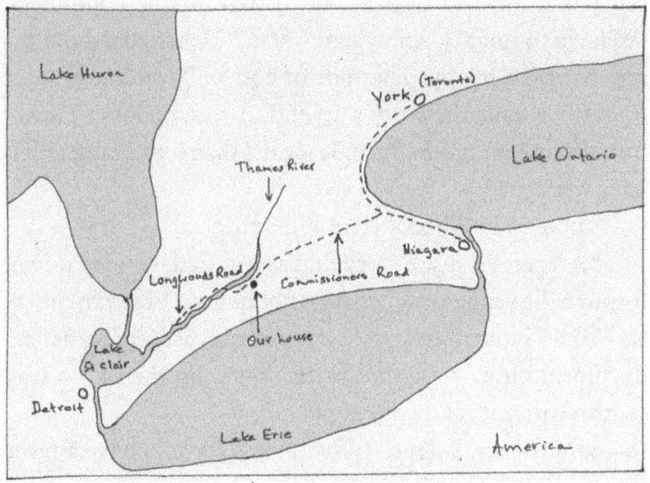

Sam looked at his dad's map. Yes, Commissioners Road was the main land route during the War of 1812. He reached for a chocolate brownie and absent-mindedly licked the icing off it. His mind was on the missing gold. But he jerked to attention when his mother spoke.

"Those musket balls that Ben and his dad found ... could they date from later than 1812? How long did muskets with musket balls last before another kind of rifle was invented?"

Parents, Sam thought. *They never let go. They're as bad as teachers. There's always one more idea, one more thing they have to point out, one more thing to look up.* He reached for another brownie.

"Let's Google it," Eadie said. "And General Procter, too."

"But we'll need to get the computers hooked up, Dad," Sam said with a grin.

"Okay, I hear you. The movers are coming tomorrow. But you'll have to wait a day or two for the computers. We have to unpack some boxes first." He stretched out his arm to reach for the Thermos of coffee. "You know, your friend Ben calls the story a legend. A legend doesn't mean that something did happen. It means that something might have happened."

Sam and Eadie looked at him, puzzled.

"A legend is just a story that's been told, handed down, through the years, which may or not be true," Liz explained.

Tom interrupted, "The problem is, there is no documentation, nothing written down. So there's no way to prove that it really did happen."

Sam was impatient. "Why do you have to have a piece of paper to make something true? Lots of things happen every day that no one writes down." He reached for a box of cookies and tore off the plastic wrapping. "Either the paymaster lost his gold or he didn't. What's so difficult about that?"

Eadie had been silent. Listening and thinking. She drew up her legs, and sat, hunched over her knees. She fiddled with her long, black hair. "If it's still a legend, then the gold has not been found."

Sam grinned. "And if we find it, then that's the end of the legend!"

Chapter Four

June 1812

The war has begun! We are at war with the United States. A Captain Rapelje came by to tell us that a militia is being formed. Father is too old, but John is the right age. He is excited about it. Cousin Ned says that he will go back to America and fight for them. That means he will be fighting against John! It's very confusing. I don't like everyone arguing.

Mother is very worried. John tells her that he will give her all his soldier's pay. Father is worried. He says that living here on Commissioner's Road, we will be exposed to the war right on our door step because this is the only road. The soldiers from both sides will use it, American and British. Lucy and I are worried. Her family is from England. We are Americans. Will we have to stop being friends?

It only took the movers one day to bring all their stuff to the house, but it took almost a week for the Jacksons to unpack and store everything away. Every day, they did nothing but carry boxes to and fro, upstairs and down. They shifted furniture around and discovered that none of their curtains fit. They lost things and found them again.

But they had lunch outside every day, on the kitchen steps by the back door. The sun shone, the breeze blew gently on their faces, and they enjoyed the long view through the old apple trees to the small woods at the back of their property. Ben dropped by a few times, and — always hungry — stayed for lunch.

Again and again, the conversation turned to the War of 1812. It was easy for Sam and Eadie and Ben to say that they would hunt for the paymaster's gold. But how? How to even begin? They had to know more about it, to figure out where to look and what exactly they were looking for. After all, the gold had been lost more than two hundred years ago.

Eadie carefully peeled a banana. "I don't understand the War of 1812. On the plaque it says that our militia fought the Americans, but I thought that Canada and the United States were always friends."

"You'll be sick of the War of 1812 if you have Old Grimshaw for history at our school." Ben reached for his fourth chocolate chip cookie and smiled slyly at Sam and Eadie's mum. "These are good!"

"Actually, in the War of 1812, Britain was fighting France, and Napoleon," Tom explained. "Have you heard of the Napoleonic Wars?"

"Yes," Sam said. He remembered a movie that he'd seen once. "Napoleon's that guy with his hand always inside his jacket."

"Well, yes, that will do, I suppose, for a description." His parents laughed.

Liz continued, "And America sold supplies to France, which helped France, and made America a lot of money. Britain didn't like that, so they blockaded France with ships so that the American ships couldn't get through."

"So," Tom continued, "that made the Americans angry so they started to beat up on Britain in Britain's colonies. And that means us, right here. It was called Upper Canada at the time. And Lower Canada — that was Quebec — and the Atlantic provinces, too."

Ben nodded. He had heard all this before, sitting in Old Grimshaw's class, but somehow it hadn't seemed so important then. But now that Sam and Eadie had moved to the neighbourhood and wanted to know more about the skirmishes on Reservoir Hill, history was much more interesting.

Sam thought about all of this and he thought about that plaque in the park. "So, what's a militia?"

Eadie got up to shake the crumbs off her jeans. Tom reached for the coffee pot. He paused, coffee pot in hand, to explain. "There would have been professional soldiers, soldiers of the king, sent out from England to defend Upper Canada. And then there would have been the militia, the local volunteers from among the settlers."

Sam wouldn't let go of the idea of the Legend of the Paymaster's Gold. "So, both the regular soldiers and the militia would need to be paid? Then there must have been lots of paymasters. So, maybe one of them did lose his gold on Commissioners Road. Maybe General Procter's paymaster. Maybe someone else's."

After gathering the dishes and leftovers, Eadie and Liz headed for the kitchen. Sam, Ben, and Tom went off to the shed-room to see what was in it and to plan how to empty it.

Finally, the computers and the printer were hooked up. Sam and Eadie started searching the Web right away. They began by looking for "paymaster" and "legend" and "gold." But they only found references to treasure buried by pirates. When they added "War of 1812," they got references to paymasters in the American military.

"Let's start again," Eadie said. "Just try 'War of 1812 and Ontario.' We don't want all the American references."

Sam stared at the computer screen. "Agghhhh! Eadie, there's 56,000 entries!"

"Let's go with the Archives of Ontario. That's the one we always use at school."

The twins scrolled on and on, down through the menus on several 1812 sites for more than an hour. There was a lot of information about Brown Bess muskets, which were what the soldiers had used during the War of 1812. And there were also images of the musket balls, slightly smaller than a modern 25-cent piece, which was in the photo for comparison.

"This is neat, Eadie. You can actually buy a replica musket and ammunition."

"And you can order bits of uniform, too. Badges and buttons."

"And look! There are re-enactment groups. Lots of them. For different regiments. That's cool. I'd like to go to one of those, watch the battle being acted out. They shoot muskets and everything."

"My eyes are falling out of my head," Sam said an hour later. "I need a break."

As a bag of popcorn popped, Sam groaned, "It's too confusing. Too many battles, too many facts to sort out. I want to hunt for the gold, not have another history lesson."

They took the popcorn to the living room and sprawled out on the floor. Eadie had made printouts of Procter's movements during the war.

"Okay, Eadie. Let's get the facts straight. General Procter was posted on the Detroit frontier with America. He got a lot of his supplies from the Niagara frontier brought in by boat on Lake Erie. He won a few battles against the Americans in Michigan, west of Detroit. Then in August of 1812, General Isaac Brock came from Niagara to help Procter and together they took Detroit from the Americans. Brock left Procter in charge of the Detroit frontier again while he went back to the Niagara frontier."

Eadie took up the story, as far as they had figured it out from their Google search. "Next, Brock got himself killed at the Battle of Queenston Heights near Niagara. Bad luck for Brock. He seemed like such a hero. They said he was very tall and handsome, and always looking for action. Remember, Sam? We saw that big monument to Brock at Queenston Heights when we went on the school trip. He was a famous leader. I like him."

"Yeah, well, I like Tecumseh, the Native leader. He was as important as General Brock. And the Natives fought on the side of the British."

Eadie got that dreamy look in her eyes. "Tecumseh seems like General Brock, tall and handsome and brave."

Sam gave Eadie a look. "You don't win wars by being handsome!"

Sam grabbed another handful of popcorn and riffled through the printouts. "The Americans were angry at having lost to Brock and Procter, so they got reinforcements.

At first, it didn't help. Procter kept winning small battles. And he kept getting promotions for that. So far, so good."

"But then it all fell apart, Sam. The Americans got more reinforcements for their army. And Procter didn't. Then the American and British navies fought a huge battle on Lake Erie. And our navy lost. With the Americans in control of the lake, Procter couldn't get supplies in to his fort."

Sam searched through the printouts and then held one up excitedly. "Fort Malden it was called."

"Right, Sam. But then the Americans came across the border at Detroit...." Eadie got to her feet.

"And everyone at the British Fort Malden was starving...."

By this time, Sam and Eadie were jumping around the living room, shouting back and forth to each other, throwing their printouts in the air.

"Procter and his Native allies were hopelessly outnumbered...."

"So Procter retreated. On boats, along Lake St. Clair and then up the Thames River. And the Americans chased him!"

"This is as good as a movie!"

"Procter and his Natives made a stand at Moraviantown, halfway between Detroit and here. And they were routed in ten minutes flat. Loads of our soldiers and Native allies were killed. Including Tecumseh."

"But this is the thing, Sam. Procter's wife and children were with him because they had been living with him at Fort Malden. Imagine! Living with him right in the war zone! What were they thinking? So Procter fled with his family ahead of his soldiers and made his way by road east along Commissioners Road, right past our house!" Eadie hunted through the printouts scattered on the floor. "That was October 6, 1813."

"Let's hope he had his gold with him, Eadie!"

"Well, his soldiers followed him. There must have been a paymaster because they had been at Fort Malden for months, and had to buy supplies from all the settlers in the district to feed the soldiers, and lots of the Natives and their families, too."

"But here's where it gets tricky, Sam." Eadie sat down on the floor again and consulted the printouts. "Procter went on ahead, but some websites say that the Americans caught up with Procter's men on Reservoir Hill. Procter's men were moving slowly because they were carrying the wounded, and some equipment and supplies."

Sam grinned at Eadie. "And maybe gold!"

Eadie reached over to a pile of books that she had set aside when she was unpacking boxes. She picked up the *History of the County of Middlesex Canada,* opened it, and she stood up straight like a soldier before reading out loud in a deep and dramatic voice, "After the Battle at Moraviantown 'General Procter retreated ... taking the Longwoods and the Commissioners Roads ... closely pursued by a small body of Kentucky riflemen.' They caught up with Captain Carroll '... who was doomed to surrender or fight. Taking the latter course, he took possession of a knoll within the great bend of the Commissioners Road.'"

"That's exactly what Reservoir Hill is like, Eadie. Even today, two hundred years later."

Eadie continued reading, "'And with Mrs. McNames, (who resided nearby) to distribute ammunition, waited the enemy's attack. The Americans, seeing a hopeless task before them, retired after one repulse.'" Eadie rummaged in the litter of printouts on the floor. "I think I read somewhere that she was Phoebe McNames."

"Hurrah for Captain Carroll! So maybe the gold was lost in the skirmish, Eadie!"

"But Sam, this is where it becomes a legend. Here's another book where it says that there is no documentary proof that there was a skirmish at all! It's just a story. But it's become the Legend of the Paymaster's Gold."

Sam grabbed the bag of popcorn. He munched on a huge handful. "It's so weird, Eadie, because lots of websites even describe the scene of the skirmish." He pulled over their father's historical atlas and read for a minute. "It says here that Carroll posted his command 'on the summit of a beautiful rounded hill, which was covered ... with a scattered growth of scrub oaks, and around which the Commissioners Road winds.' It's so crazy, that's right here! What can you believe? And what about Phoebe McNames? Did she help the soldiers or not?"

Eadie was silent. She lined up ten kernels of popcorn in a row on the edge of the coffee table. Then she ate them slowly, one by one. "All that means nothing, Sam, if there's no official record that it ever happened. These are only stories."

"But, Eadie, why would people tell stories about the skirmish if it never happened? There must be a zillion things that happen every day that nobody writes down." Sam made a paper airplane out of a printout and sent it flying across the room. "But those things still happened."

Eadie gathered up the printouts as Sam reached for the popcorn bag to finish off the last crumbs. "Look, Sam, even if there wasn't a skirmish on Reservoir Hill, supposing General Procter just hurried by and Captain Carroll just plodded along with his wounded and his baggage wagons, we still know that they had gold with them. Which could have been lost. Or maybe they were afraid that the Americans might catch up with them so they hid the gold. And Procter's troops weren't the only troops that passed this way during the war. There was a lot of military traffic. And maybe other paymasters with gold. Think of that plaque in the park. That little skirmish a year after Procter's retreat, when Captain Carroll was killed. Maybe the American raiders had gold with them. Maybe they had looted it from Canadian settlers. Maybe it was lost in the skirmish.

"If there's any truth in any of this, someone, somewhere, lost or hid some gold on Commissioners Road near Reservoir Hill. Even if it wasn't General Procter's paymaster's gold."

Sam grinned. "Absolutely! There's got to be somebody's gold on Reservoir Hill. We've just got to find it!"

Chapter Five

November 1812

The war is so exciting — soldiers march past on the road in red uniforms with guns and gun carriages. The Indians are fighting on our side. Captain Carroll came today and told Father that our General Isaac Brock has been killed at Queenston by the Americans. Imagine if a battle like that was fought right here, between our place and the Tuckers'! If that happened, Mother and I would hide in the cellar and take our silver spoons with us.

The next morning, when Sam got up, he wanted to get on his bike, find Ben, and go explore the scene of the legendary skirmish and legendary loss of the legendary gold. Maybe Ben would even bring his dad's metal detector. Sam was fed up with unpacking from the move. He went downstairs, hungry for breakfast.

His father was just leaving for work. "Your mother and I want to get started on the shed-room. I've arranged for the builder to come tomorrow to see if it's possible to knock a door through to it from the kitchen, to make it more part of the house. I want it cleared out before he arrives. So, will you and your sister get busy on that today? Just put everything in the garage for now. Some of the odd pieces of lumber might come in handy. And we'll definitely want to keep the firewood."

"But —" Sam started to protest.

Eadie shot Sam a warning look from across the table.

"Okay, Dad," Sam said.

Their parents didn't take the story of the paymaster's gold seriously, but Sam and Eadie and Ben did. They all thought that the gold really went missing. When they decided to search for it, they also decided not to tell their parents. It was best to keep their heads down and not argue.

Sam lingered over an extra waffle at breakfast. Finally, he couldn't delay any longer. He went upstairs and changed into his oldest clothes: a stained and faded green T-shirt and some seriously ripped jeans. He joined Eadie in the shed-room. She had put on a torn blue shirt and paint-spattered jeans, and she'd tied a red scarf over her long, dark hair. "This place is filthy, Sam. This is going to be an 'Ugh' job."

"If we were sixteen," Sam grumbled, "we could get a paid summer job. But no, we have to do all this work for Mum and Dad and never get paid a cent."

Eadie sighed. "I was hoping to get some babysitting jobs this summer but I don't know any of the families around here, so that's not going to happen."

They continued working in gloomy silence, shifting old pieces of filthy lumber. Everything they touched threw up clouds of dust: broken chairs, broken screens for windows, boxes of rags. And mouse droppings. Lots of mouse droppings. They kept the door propped open but still the dust was choking them. They had to tie scarves over their noses to stop themselves from sneezing.

After a few hours, they heard Liz call, "Sam! Eadie! Get cleaned up for lunch now. Take a break."

"Has Ben been here?" Sam asked his mother.

"No. I saw him painting their fence a little while ago."

Sam and Eadie looked at each other. Ben's day was turning out to be as bad as theirs!

After lunch, as the shed-room emptied out, Sam and Eadie could see its size better. It was as big as the living room. They could also see that there were umpteen layers of old linoleum on the floor.

"You'll have to rip all that floor covering up," Liz said. "If we're lucky, there may be a decent wood floor underneath."

Sam and Eadie toiled on. They ripped out layers and layers of linoleum and carried it outside to make a huge pile under a tree. Underneath the linoleum there was indeed a wooden floor. Some of the planks were very wide, at least thirty centimetres across. They were impressed. And so was their mother.

"What a lovely floor this could be, once it's cleaned up. Look at those floorboards. They must be very old. It would take big old trees to yield planks that width."

Sam tore out another big, scummy brown piece of linoleum. "Hey, Eadie. Look at this! There's a trap door!"

He wanted to lift the trap door to investigate but his mother stopped him.

"Goodness knows what's down there," she said. "Could be anything! Mould and decaying animals and cobwebs, even rats. Dad will be home soon. We can explore it then. We'll need flashlights. See if you can find them in all this muddle of unpacking."

"But, Mum ..."

"No 'buts.' Wait for Dad."

But when Tom got home, they had to wait for supper.

Then they had to wait through supper.

Then they had to wait until Tom finished his coffee and changed into old clothes. Because the cellar would be filthy, of course.

Finally, Tom lifted the trap door and peered down into the hole. He switched on the flashlight. "It's definitely a cellar. But I can't see how big it is. I'll need a ladder to get down there."

"Wait, Dad," Sam said. "We found a ladder today. It's in the garage. We'll get it." Sam and Eadie ran off to get the ladder.

When they returned with it, Tom placed it carefully down the cellar hole and stepped down into the darkness. "It's just a root cellar, I think. It's very small," he called out to the others waiting above.

Sam and Eadie wanted to see it, too. They clambered down the ladder. They both had flashlights. Sam flashed his around to get a better look. The cellar was like a cave. There was no floor, just earth. And the walls were earth, too. It wasn't square, just a hole dug out unevenly. And not very big. They could only take five or six steps in each direction. And the ceiling beams weren't very high up, either. Tom couldn't stand upright and had to stoop. When Eadie pointed her flashlight above their heads, she could see the big rough beams that held up the floor of the shed-room. They looked like whole tree trunks. She reached up her hand to feel them, their roughness. Tom warned them not to poke around in the corners, but that is exactly what they wanted to do! He made them go up the ladder again.

"You've had a look. That's enough," he declared.

"But, Dad ..."

Tom lowered the trap door, stamped it shut, and turned to Sam and Eadie. "I don't want you two going down there. It's filthy. Leave it alone. That's an order."

The twins went upstairs to Eadie's room to talk it over.

"The cellar is a perfect place to hide something, Eadie. If we could get Ben's metal detector down in there...."

"That's not going to happen, Sam. Dad's not going to let us down there again."

"It's so unfair, Eadie. A little bit of dirt never hurt anyone."

"The shed-room is so weird, Sam. With those big tree trunks for beams that we saw in the cellar, I think it might have been a log cabin once."

"That's crazy, Eadie."

"Not really. It seems like part of the house from the outside but it's not."

Eadie took a piece of paper and a pencil and quickly drew a floor plan of their house.

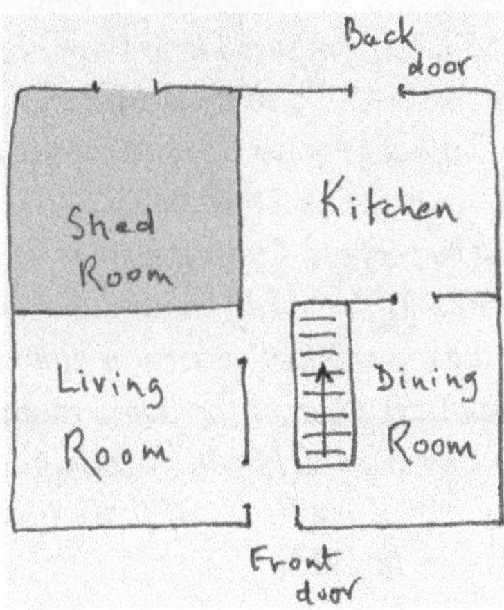

"See, Sam? That shed-room is one quarter of the house. But you can only get into it from outside. And it has a dirt cellar, but the rest of the house has a more proper basement with a cement floor and everything."

"Do you think it was part of a cabin that was here in 1812? Could the gold be hidden in the shed-room? Or the cellar?"

"I don't know, Sam. We can't ask that lady who lived here before us, Mrs. Foster, because she's gone away to Australia for months and months."

Sam flung himself down on Eadie's bed. "This is all crazy. Why would anyone build a new house around an old log cabin?"

"Don't know. It doesn't make sense."

That night, Sam sprawled on his bed, thinking about the trap door and the cellar. *What a perfect place to hide a bag of gold!* But, at the same time, he had nagging doubts. *Of course, if there was a paymaster, and if he hid his gold — say, to keep it safe during a skirmish — the cellar would be a perfect place. But then the cellar would have to have been here in 1813. But I'm sure I heard Mrs. Foster say this house was built in 1865. So that's a dead end.*

Eadie sat on the edge of her bed and considered the shed-room. Her mind was racing. She thought of the possibilities. *That room must be very old. Older than the rest of the house. Those floorboards in the shed-room are so wide, as wide as the ones in the log cabins I've seen in pioneer museums. It's different from the floor in the living room. That's just ordinary narrow hardwood. Maybe the shed-room was built earlier than the rest of the house. If that's true, maybe the shed-room was here in 1813!*

Chapter Six

October 1813

I have not written in my journal for so long. Every day is just work and more work. But last night there was great excitement! The war came to us! There was shouting on the road and gunshots on the hill. Father made Mother and I hide in the cellar and I took our silver spoons with us, wrapped in a blanket. Father and John went to investigate. They didn't come back until this morning. They told us that General Procter lost a battle with the Americans at Moraviantown, west of here. Last night he was retreating eastward along our road and some Kentucky Riflemen caught up with him on the hill. General Procter escaped and brave Captain Carroll fended off the Americans. Some of the wounded were taken to Tuckers'. Father said that some of the wagons were damaged and some baggage was lost.

Now that the British soldiers have gone to Niagara, there is only the militia to protect us against raids by the Americans. Mother is terrified.

The next morning, the builders phoned to say that they couldn't come that day and probably would not start work on the shed-room for a week or two. Ben phoned to say that he'd run out of paint, so he was free of painting the fence for a day. Liz told the twins to take the day off as well. The weather was perfect for searching for gold.

"Let's visit the scene of the crime!" Ben suggested when he arrived at Sam and Eadie's house.

"The crime?"

"Yeah, you know, a re-enactment. Let's re-enact the skirmish on Reservoir Hill, with Procter hurrying east and Captain Carroll fending off the Americans. We might get some ideas about where to look for the gold."

"Perfect," said Sam.

So they set off, on their bikes, and headed west on Commissioners Road. In less than three minutes they were peering down Reservoir Hill. It was a steep descent to the Thames River valley below. Halfway down the hill was a hairpin bend, the road turning first to the left and then to the right. It turned so sharply that they couldn't see cars coming up the hill.

Sam and Eadie told Ben what they had found on the Internet. Everything they had read was starting to make sense. Eadie reached into her knapsack for her notebook. "Look, here's two different descriptions we found." She read them out to the boys, "That huge Goodspeed book says 'the knoll within the great bend of Commissioners

Road.' And Dad's historical atlas has 'the rounded hill ... round which the Commissioners Road winds.'"

From where they stood, it looked exactly the same today, two hundred years later: the steep hill, the winding road.

"It's amazing," said Sam. "It all fits. Just like 1813 when General Procter and Captain Carroll came by."

They pretended that they were General Procter, Captain Carroll, and the group of soldiers and wounded struggling up the hill. When they looked back down the hill they realized that because of the sharp bends the soldiers would not have been able to see the Kentucky Riflemen chasing after them and getting closer and closer.

They imagined General Procter heading up the hill as fast he could, travelling lightly, anxious to get his wife and children to safety. And then, later, brave Captain Carroll trying to get horses and baggage wagons and wounded men manoeuvred up the twisting hill, all the while knowing the Americans were coming up the hill behind them. And Captain Carroll turning to fend the Americans off.

"This hill is really difficult," said Sam.

"I'd hate to have been Captain Carroll," said Ben. "He would have had to turn around, maybe block the road with his wagons, to defend himself." Ben had obviously been doing some online searching, too. "Did you know that Procter got court-martialled?"

"No. What's that?"

"It's a court. The army had its own court."

"What did he do wrong? He won all those battles in Michigan...."

"It was because of his retreat. Right here, on Commissioners Road. He wasn't blamed for retreating, because his supply line was cut and he was outnumbered by the Americans. But they said that he did a lousy job of organizing the retreat. He didn't take care to burn the bridges across the Thames River after he had crossed them. He didn't build any defences at Moraviantown. Not even abatis." Ben explained when he saw the confusion on the twins' faces. "Those are piles of brushwood made into a wall to hide behind. He also abandoned his troops in the field after the battle and he abandoned his Native allies, too. That's when he just tore off eastward and along Commissioners Road past here."

"Wow! After all the good stuff he did, to lose it in the end." Sam shook his head. "One mistake and he lost his whole career."

"Yeah. Pretty bad, eh?"

"Maybe, in the end, he forgot that he was a soldier, and just became a dad looking after his family, getting them to safety," Eadie said.

But the boys rounded on her. "You can't abandon more than 600 soldiers and 1,000 Native allies, Eadie!

Ben propped his bike against his knee and reached to open his knapsack. With his red hair and fair skin, he sunburned easily. He took out his sunscreen and slathered it all over his arms and legs. Then they hauled their bikes up above the tight bend in the road and parked them against the steep banks.

"Race you to the top!" Ben shouted.

They scrambled up the bank. It was tough going: slippery with leaf litter, scratchy with wild roses. They had to grab the trunks of shrubs to keep from falling backwards, and they had to brace their feet against the tree trunks to keep their balance. Sam got a huge scratch on his arm, which oozed blood. Ben cracked his knee against a rock and it began to swell. Eadie's legs and knees were covered with dirt from scrabbling in the dead leaves and earth at the base of the trees.

Once at the top of the bank, they flopped on the grass.

Ben inspected his swollen knee. "These banks are really steep! Good to defend but hard to attack. I guess that's why the Kentucky Riflemen gave up so easily."

Sam and Ben discussed the range that a musket could fire — about 100 yards but only accurate to about 75 yards. They moved back from the bank to estimate the range but then they decided that the range didn't really matter since you had to be right at the edge of the bank to see down into the ravine to the road below, anyway.

Eadie looked around at the bushes and trees. "I wonder how many trees were here in 1813? Were they big like the ones in Reservoir Park? I mean, how could General Procter's men see through the trees to shoot the Americans in the road below?"

"Don't know," Sam said. "They were shooting in the dark, too." He opened his knapsack. "I'm hungry."

Sam and Eadie pulled out the sandwiches and drinks from their knapsacks and shared with Ben. Ham, peanut butter and banana, Potato chips, pop, and chocolate chip cookies.

"No carrot sticks!" Sam said gleefully.

"We packed the lunch ourselves," Eadie told Ben.

He laughed. "Mothers!"

After they had stuffed themselves, they sprawled lazily on the grass (in the shade, for Ben's sake). They talked about the War of 1812, the skirmish on Reservoir Hill, and the lost gold. Then Sam and Eadie described their shed-room to Ben and how it had no door through to the rest of the house.

"But the weirdest thing is, it's got a trap door with a cellar down below. And it's dug out, like a cave. We went down there with Dad last night. It would be a great place to hide gold...."

"But," Ben said skeptically, "was it there in 1813 when Procter passed by?"

Sam sighed. "Well, Mrs. Foster told us that our house was built in 1865."

"Bummer."

Eadie listened, but said nothing. She had her own theory about the shed-room. She smiled to herself and reached for another cookie.

Eventually the conversation drifted to school. The twins asked Ben about his high school, the one that they would be going to in September. They liked what they heard: lots of sports, a cool math teacher, a fantastic geography teacher, a music programme where they were allowed any music they liked — even rap — and a good art program. Maybe they would survive after all — even survive the notorious Old Grimshaw — although they would still miss their friends at their old school.

Ben got to his feet, his swollen knee forgotten. "Come on. Let's do a re-enactment. I went to one last year. It was of the Battle of Longwoods. That's the War of 1812, too, and that was about eighty kilometres west of here. They had muskets and cannons and everything."

"But we'll do General Procter and Captain Carroll today," Eadie said.

"I'll be the British soldiers here on top of the bank. First of all, I'll cover General Procter who is hurrying off up the hill ahead of the others. Then I'll give cover for Captain Carroll as he struggles to organize the carts with the wounded and the baggage wagons up the hill out of harm's way. Sam, you be the Americans, chasing Proctor's party."

"And I'll be the paymaster," Eadie said proudly.

Sam set off, scrambling down the bank to the road. Ben, as British soldiers on top of the bank, gave a whoop and started shouting at him, pretending to fire his musket. Sam ran along the road up the hill, pretending to dodge Ben's bullets. Eadie didn't know what to do. She stood still at the top of the bank, undecided.

"Come on, Eadie," the boys shouted.

"Listen. We've got a problem," she shouted back. She and Ben stumbled down the bank, hanging onto trees to keep themselves from slipping. They met up with Sam in the road. Ben was limping.

"You see," Eadie explained, "if there was a paymaster here, where would he be? Would he be up on that bank, shooting at the Americans down on the road? Or would he be hidden away, guarding his gold, so the Americans wouldn't get it? And if he lost his gold, how did he lose it? Did he drop it? Did he hide it? Did he get killed? If he didn't get killed, did he come back for the gold later?"

Silence. They each considered what Eadie had said.

Eadie bent over to pick up her bike. "We figured out where General Procter's skirmish took place, here, on Reservoir Hill, when Captain Carroll fended off the Kentucky Riflemen. But we don't know any more about paymasters or their gold."

They walked their bikes slowly, zigzagging up the hill, thinking about the skirmish — if it had ever taken place.

When they reached the top, Sam shouted "Race you!" and climbed on his bike. He set off along Commissioners Road. Ben had to screw the top on his sunscreen tube and throw it in his bag, and Eadie had to tie her shoelace, so Sam had a big head start. Ben and Eadie could see him up ahead.

Then they heard a racket. A pack of dogs bounded across a field, then through a hole in the fence next to the road. Barking like crazy, the four dogs ran after Sam's bike. They were black and white collies, circling with excitement and snapping their jaws. Sam lifted his feet up toward the handle bars but the dogs kept after him. Sam headed for a fencepost and grabbed it so that he could stay on top of his bike and keep his feet up while the dogs jumped around him.

"Those are Old Tucker's dogs," Ben said. He and Eadie had stopped and were standing beside their bikes, trying not to draw the dogs' attention.

Ben bellowed, "Mr. Tucker! Mr. Tucker! Call off your dogs!" A few minutes later, they heard a shout and the dogs slunk back along the fence and through the hole back into the field.

Sam was pale and shaken. "What a fool. He can't let his dogs run loose like that!"

"Maybe not in the city," Ben said. "But this is the country. And Old Tucker is a miserable guy. He's no fun. He won't let anyone on his property."

Eadie sighed. Now, every time they took their bikes on the road, they'd have to look out for Old Tucker's dogs and maybe even Old Tucker himself.

Chapter Seven

October 12, 1813

Lucy Tucker told me an amazing thing today. She said that Mrs. McNames, who lives farther east along Commissioner's Road, was actually caught in the skirmish on the hill the other night when General Procter was fleeing to Niagara!! A lady was having a baby and sent her son to find Mrs. McNames to help. They were heading west down the hill when they met Captain Carroll halfway up, preparing to defend his wagons and the wounded against the American Kentucky Riflemen. She sent the boy to Tuckers' to be safe. She was trapped with our soldiers. She helped them load their muskets. Lucy and I think that she was terribly brave. Today, Captain Carroll came back with a posse of men and they tramped all over our place and the Greenaways' and Tuckers' looking for something. Father thinks that they were looking for something valuable that was lost in the skirmish. Lucy and I are going to search tomorrow. Maybe there will be a reward. Lucy's father says that the paymaster carries a lot of money in a wooden box with a lock. The mother had the baby and they are fine.

Another week went by. Liz had taken two weeks of holiday from work to deal with the move, but now she was back at work and Sam and Eadie were on their own all day. Some days she gave them instructions about odd jobs and errands to do, and sometimes not. But they always had to phone her at lunch time. As far as the twins were concerned, that was perfect. It was easy to tell their mum that they were fine, that they were fooling around on their bikes with Ben. Their parents didn't believe in the paymaster's gold. Besides, the twins would rather solve the legend by themselves. With Ben, of course.

In fact, they usually weren't even lying when they said that they were fooling around on their bikes. Ben took Sam and Eadie on long bike rides to explore the neighbourhood. They found a baseball diamond and a regular schedule of games to watch, which pleased Sam. There were tennis courts, too, and Eadie learned that there were lessons offered in the mornings, for different skill levels. She decided to sign up for lessons later in the summer. Best of all, there was Springbank Park. It was more than 100 years old. Sam and Eadie had visited it when they lived in the city, but that had been by car. They had never explored it on their bikes before.

The park was all lawns and huge, old, shady trees. Eadie could imagine Victorian picnics there. She had seen photographs in books: elegant ladies in long, lacy dresses, holding parasols to keep off the sun; little boys playing chase in their sailor suits; gentlemen with moustaches, side whiskers, and their cigars. The park stretched all the way to London along the bank of the Thames River, more than seven kilometres.

There were other interesting things about Springbank, especially when considering its name: *spring bank*. The springs flowing down the bank from the Reservoir Hill to the Thames River had been harnessed into a water-supply system for the City of London in 1878. The water was pumped up to the reservoir at the top of the hill. Sam and Eadie had read about that on the plaque in Reservoir Park. In Springbank Park, they saw the original pumphouse, which was designed to look like a cottage, sitting squat beside the beautiful river.

But there was tragedy in the park, too. Ben showed Sam and Eadie the plaque that commemorated the *Victoria* Boat Disaster. River cruises on steamboats were a popular holiday activity. On May 24, 1881, the steamboat *Victoria* capsized on the Thames River, right in Springbank Park. One hundred and eighty-two people lost their lives. More than half of them were children. The boat had been grossly overloaded. And it was probably also top-heavy. It turned over suddenly, wrecking the superstructure of the boat, which became a tangled mess, trapping the passengers in the water. There were terrible stories: the deaths, the lack of sufficient coffins in the town for the number of dead children, the churches busy with funerals all day long. Ben and Sam and Eadie looked at the site where the *Victoria* had turned over, and thought about the chaos and tragedy that day more than 100 years earlier.

But the Legend of the Paymaster's Gold was never far from their minds. They talked about it endlessly and threw a lot of ideas around. They decided that they needed to do more research.

"Let's check out the library. Your mum said that it had some good stuff about the War of 1812, Ben."

The local library, in a small building all by itself, was just like the other libraries Sam and Eadie knew. However, it had one big surprise: the librarian. He was very tall, very thin, very tattooed, and very pierced.

"Hi, guys. I'm Dave. What can I do for you?"

He had a big smile and seemed friendly enough. Sam and Ben said that they wanted to search on the computer.

"Carry on," said Dave. "If you need help, shout." They were going to try to find out more about paymasters. They wanted to know if paymasters travelled with troops or just worked from an office in some headquarters somewhere. Even if General Procter's skirmish on Reservoir Hill was only a legend, they knew that it was true that he had retreated from Moraviantown east along Commissioners Road. The question was: did he have a paymaster with him? They were also curious as to what soldiers got paid. If they were looking for paymasters' gold, how much gold would there be?

Eadie settled down at a table with Dave. She told him that she wanted to find out something about early settlers. Had anybody built a log cabin in the area by 1812? Like, maybe, Phoebe McNames? She told Dave about the Legend of the Paymaster's Gold.

Dave smiled. "That's a well-known story, Eadie. Can't help you, though. I guess that will be a legend until proved otherwise." He thought for a moment. "But I've got something that might interest you." He brought out a big file of typed sheets. “This is the transcript of an Ontario Municipal Board hearing.”

Eadie knew what the Ontario Municipal Board was because her dad, as a city planner, often talked about “OMB decisions.” When citizens objected to a planning decision, they could argue their case to the provincial Ontario Municipal Board to seek to change the decision.

“A developer wanted to build some condos at the edge of Reservoir Hill. They would be on private land, mind you, but they would overlook Springbank Park,” Dave explained. “A heritage group argued against the condos and one of their arguments was that the Reservoir Hill is a historic site because of General Procter and Captain Carroll and that skirmish.”

“Was that the Save the Reservoir Hill Group?” Eadie asked, remembering the plaque in Reservoir Park.

“You’re right. But you should read these transcripts, Eadie, because the people who wanted to build the condos argued just the opposite: that the skirmish never happened. It’s just a legend. There was no documentary or archaeological evidence.”

“But Ben — he’s sitting over there at the computer — he found musket balls with his metal detector! Right on Reservoir Hill!”

“But were those musket balls from the legendary skirmish? There was an ambush on Reservoir Hill in 1814, and in 1913 there was a re-enactment of the skirmish and they fired muskets then.”

Eadie sighed. She remembered what her mother had said about the musket balls that Ben had found. How did they really know that they dated from the War of 1812?

“This is sounding worse and worse. Who did the Ontario Municipal Board believe?”

"The Board works on evidence. And there is no documentary evidence to say that General Procter's skirmish ever happened."

"So they threw out the heritage group's argument?"

"'Fraid so."

Eadie sighed again. "What about Phoebe McNames then? Is she a legend, too? Did she really live on Commissioners Road?"

Dave brought out some old maps. On one of them Eadie could see the name *McNames* on Commissioners Road.

"Oh, so there really was a family called McNames!"

"Absolutely. You can go to the Brick Street Cemetery and see some of the McNameses' gravestones."

"So, is the story of Phoebe McNames helping the soldiers on Reservoir Hill true?"

"'Fraid not, Eadie. If there was no skirmish, how could Phoebe be passing the ammunition to the soldiers?"

Eadie slumped in her chair. Legends, she decided, were nothing but disappointment. No skirmish on Reservoir Hill, no Phoebe McNames to the rescue.

Eadie had one more question for Dave. She was thinking about early settlers.

"How many people were living on Commissioners Road at Reservoir Hill in 1812?"

Dave brought out a historic atlas and several more maps. "The McNameses weren't the only families living in the area at the time." He pointed at the map. "See: Fairchild, McMillen, Wareham, Kilbourn, Sutherland, and Tucker."

Tucker! Eadie remembered Old Tucker and his dogs. *Imagine his family having been here from the beginning of settlement!*

"In fact, Eadie, there is still a Tucker on the original family property. That's up on Reservoir Hill," Dave continued. "It's hard to know who was here in 1812 with any accuracy because people came and squatted on the land and only applied for their official land grants years later. Some of them came for a few years and then left without a trace. We will never know who they were."

"What did a settler have to do to become 'official'?"

"He had to fulfil four conditions of settlement: (1) build a house at least 16 feet by 20 feet, (2) clear 10 acres of land of trees, (3) clear half the width of the roadway in front of his property — the settlers had to build the roads, you understand — and, (4) clear all the trees 100 feet from the road back into their property."

Eadie closed the atlas and straightened the maps. She said to herself, "At least I know that there were families living on Commissioners Road and in the area during the War of 1812. Even Old Tucker's family was here. They've been here for 200 years! They'd have built log houses and they could have been hiding places for the gold."

But Dave was still talking. "Mind you, the early settlers had a rough time during the War of 1812. The men had to serve in the militia and there was no one left at home to plant or harvest the crops. And after General Procter retreated back toward Niagara, there was no protection for anyone in the London district against Americans raiding across from Detroit. Andrew Westbrook, have you heard of him? He was one of the most well-known raiders."

"We read about him on the plaque in Reservoir Park."

"That's him. He caused a lot of settlers a lot of trouble."

"I wish that someone had written a diary back then, describing the war."

"That's too easy, Eadie. History takes work. Detective work." Dave gathered up the maps and took them away.

Eadie had an idea. She took her notebook out of her knapsack and wrote down the four conditions of settlement. Then she drew a cabin 16 by 20 feet square. Then she drew a road. She labelled the distance from the road to the cabin as 100 feet. "I'm going to check this out," she said to herself.

Sam and Ben had abandoned the computers. Eadie found them outside the library, sitting on a bench. Ben was busy digging into his knapsack for sunscreen. Sam had a drink in his hand. But they had some printouts, so they must had found something. She found an energy bar in her knapsack and sat down beside them to tell them her news.

"Officially, General Procter's skirmish is still a legend, at least according to the Ontario Municipal Board."

"Who cares about that," Sam said. "We know that Procter moved along Commissioners Road with his troops and we know that Procter really did have some gold with him. It doesn't matter if there was a skirmish on Reservoir Hill or not. We just care about the gold. Procter could have lost it, or hidden it, even if there was no skirmish with the Americans."

"How much gold did he have?" Eadie asked.

"That depends," Ben said. He shuffled through some printouts. "The paymasters mostly stayed in their headquarters. They didn't go off fighting with the troops. But they did have to get pay to the soldiers from time to time, either taking it themselves or getting a senior officer to take it."

"So sometimes paymasters were wandering around the countryside, delivering gold to pay the soldiers?" Eadie asked.

"Right. And sometimes to pay farmers for the use of their horses or wagons for a few days. We saw on this website, called *War of 1812,* that the paymaster had a box three feet long and 18 inches wide to keep his stuff in: the money, his account books, and paper and ink, and his clothes. The box had handles for carrying and it had a padlock."

Sam picked up one of the printouts. "Here it says that a paymaster in New Brunswick ran out of money so he went along to a paymaster in another district to bring back money to his office." He shuffled his papers. "And, in another story, a paymaster had to get gold to a company of soldiers, to pay them, but he couldn't go himself. So he sent a soldier with it. The soldier took the money, deserted the army, and got across the border to the United States!"

They all laughed.

"I've got another story," said Ben. "I don't know whether it's about a paymaster or not, but it shows that there was gold travelling around, so it could have been lost, or hidden. This is a letter from one soldier to his brother. I'll read it to you. It's from the official Ontario Archives site. It was written in 1813, so it sounds a bit funny, the way it's written. But you'll get the picture: 'We've had a most harassing journey of 10 days to this place when we arrived last night in a snow storm. It has been snowing all day and is now a half foot deep.... Frequently I had to go ... deep in a mud hole and unload the wagon and carry heavy trunks waist deep in the mire and reload the wagon. Sometimes put my shoulder to the forewheel and raise it up.'

"Now I'm getting to the good part," Ben said. "'One night the wagon (upset) going up a steep hill in the woods in one of the worst places I ever saw.... I carried the load up to the top whilst Mr. Couche rode on 3 miles in the rain for a lanthorn ...'"

"I bet that means a lantern," Eadie interjected.

Ben continued, "'And about 11 o'clock we got it when we missed a trunk with 500 guineas ... in it. Mr. Couche and I immediately rode back 2 miles and found it in a mud hole but nothing lost....'"

Sam grinned. "So, you see? People did lose gold back then!"

Ben laughed, "But in this case, they found it again!"

Eadie was amazed. "Five hundred guineas! They don't use guineas anymore. Only pounds."

"Yeah. Let's say £500 then. Keep it simple. And let's say a pound is worth two dollars, although it changes up and down all the time. That's $1,000, more or less."

"How much did a soldier get paid?"

Sam looked at his notes. "The officers got a lot more than the men. But there weren't many officers. The men got about a shilling a day, both regular soldiers and local militia."

Ben smoothed out a printout and turned it over to its blank side. "Got a pencil, Eadie?" He began to make some calculations. "Procter had 600 soldiers at Moraviantown. Let's say that each soldier got one shilling a day. So every day, that would be 600 shillings to pay out. Suppose the soldiers get paid every six months. That's just a guess. It's not as though they worked in one place, nine to five. Six months is 182 days. So 182 days at 600 shillings a day is 109,200 shillings!"

"That sounds like a lot," said Sam, "but it's only shillings. We have to convert it to pounds. Twenty shillings to a pound."

"Right. So 109,200 shillings divided by twenty gives £5,460."

"And at two dollars for each pound, that's more than $10,000!"

"That's amazing!"

"That's worth going for!"

Chapter Eight

October 25, 1813

Everything is going wrong. Cousin Ned is in America fighting against us. John has been ordered to go to fight at Niagara and Thomas Greenaway is going with him. Father is at his wit's end. There is no one to help him with the heavy work. And a fox got into the chickens and killed four last night. Mother is so worried. One good thing is that Lucy and I can still be friends because John is fighting for the British and that pleases Lucy's family because they are from England.

The weather is very cold.

A few days later, Ben arrived with his metal detector. Sam and Eadie collected a spade, several trowels, and a bucket, and they set off for Reservoir Hill. Eadie brought along her camera. She wanted to record the moment when they found the gold.

"It's not the cheapest machine and it's not the most expensive one," Ben explained. The metal detector was not very big or heavy. It looked like a wand. "But it hunts down to a depth of thirty centimetres or so and it can detect gold."

When the trio got to Reservoir Hill, Sam put his mind to work, imagining General Procter's soldiers struggling up the hill with Captain Carroll and taking a stand against the Americans who were catching them up from behind. "If there was a paymaster with a box of gold," he reckoned, "he would have left the road, and climbed up out of the ravine to the fields at the top, to get out of the way of the fighting on the road."

"Right," Ben said. "So we stay on the top of the hill and try the fields on the north side of the road. We can keep the metal detector's discrimination at low. There won't be much junk in this field, probably no drink cans. It can pick up gold, silver, brass, lead, and copper."

Sam was impressed.

Ben held the metal detector and Sam and Eadie walked beside him. He began at the edge of the field near the road and walked slowly back and forth, sweeping the metal detector in broad strokes in front of him. It was like mowing a lawn. They gradually worked their way back from the road into the middle of the field.

At first it was exciting when the metal detector beeped. Sam and Eadie did the digging: some nails from the old fences, fence wire, and fence staples. They also found a rusty horseshoe. Ben was thrilled when they found an arrowhead — not from the metal detector because the arrowhead was made of stone. They turned it up while digging for something else. By the time they had finished with the field, they had unearthed five musket balls.

Eadie's eyes were shining with excitement. She kept peering up and down the field, and back toward the edge of the ravine and the hairpin bend in the road. "Can't you imagine it! Captain Carroll standing here, firing on the Kentucky Riflemen and trying to haul the wounded out of harm's way."

Ben was caught up in Eadie's excitement. "And everyone cheering when the Americans backed off down the hill."

Finding the musket balls right where the legendary skirmish took place made it all so real.

"This proves it's definitely not a legend," Sam said, holding out a fist full of musket balls. "You can prove lots of things without having them written in official documents."

"Absolutely! Like archaeologists do," Ben agreed, wiping the sweat off his face. "Let's take a break. I need some shade." They collapsed in the grass under shady trees at the edge of the field. Ben reached for his sunscreen. It was so hot that there were no birds around — they must have been resting in the shade, too.

After a while, Sam got to his feet, ready for more work with the metal detector. "Let's do that field on the south side of the road now." He slapped at the grasshoppers jumping at his legs.

"No way," Ben said. "That's Old Tucker's land. He won't let anyone on it. He never lets Dad and me take the metal detector on that field."

"Why not?" Sam was indignant.

"Just because. He's like that."

"What a creep. What's the good of searching the field on this side of the road if you can't search the field on the other side of the road? The gold could be in either one. That gives us only a 50 percent chance of finding it." Sam kicked at a stone and sent it flying.

Ben shrugged. He'd had run-ins with Old Tucker before. He was a crabby old man on a run-down farm, with fiercely protective dogs. Ben wasn't prepared to push it.

"Tucker is one of the original pioneer families. I saw it on the maps in the library. The Tuckers were here by 1812," Eadie piped up.

"Old family. Old grump," was Ben's only comment.

There didn't seem much else they could do. All their hopes that the metal detector would find the gold were dashed. And Old Tucker just didn't seem fair.

Eadie stood up and reached into her knapsack. She pulled out her notebook and opened it to the map she had drawn at the library. "I've got another idea."

Sam and Ben peered at the sketch map over her shoulder.

"Dave at the library said that there were four conditions of settlement for when a settler could apply for the grant to his land from the government. The first two conditions don't matter so much to us, that he had to help clear the road and clear trees. But we could use the other two conditions. The settler had to build a log house 16 by 20 feet, and it had to be 100 feet back from the road. I've drawn that here, see? I've made it to scale."

She pointed at the sketch map. "See, these are the measurements. We could take a line 100 feet from the road and follow it parallel to the road through the fields. Say from our house west toward the top of Reservoir Hill. The log cabins would have been built along that line. We can't see them now because they were torn down years ago, but the metal detector might pick up some old bits of metal, like a spoon or a buckle or a horseshoe, where the cabins used to be!"

"Or a coin!"

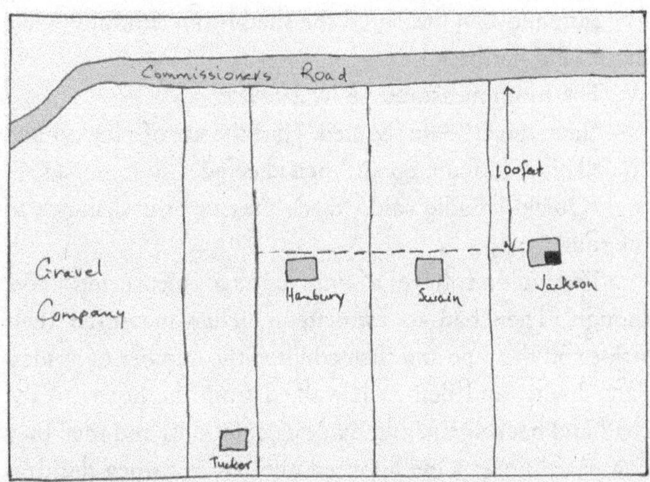

"Right. And we can look for any patterns on the ground which give a 16 by 20 foot rectangle. Maybe an old foundation...?"

"I see," Ben said slowly. "We should ignore the newer houses along the road, then, so we can find the old pioneer pattern of houses."

"You sound just like Dave," Eadie laughed.

Sam and Ben looked at each other. Eadie waited.

Finally, they both exclaimed, "Brilliant, Eadie!"

"Where do we start?"

Eadie grinned. "Well, our shed-room doesn't make any sense. It's not connected with the rest of the house, so maybe it was built first, maybe even by 1812! And then the rest of the house was built around it in 1865. Think about those wide floorboards, like the ones at pioneer museums."

"A log cabin!" Sam exclaimed.

"Let's go!" Ben said, picking up his metal detector.

They walked back along Commissioners Road to Sam and Eadie's house. Sam got their dad's measuring tape.

Sam and Ben measured the shed-room carefully while Eadie held her breath.

The room measured 16 by 20 feet!

"Incredible!" Sam shouted. "Just the size of a log cabin."

"This is looking good!" Ben cheered.

"Quick!" Eadie said. "Let's measure the distance to the road."

They didn't have a long enough measuring tape, though. They had to estimate it. They measured their strides on the tape and then counted the number of strides. Sam, Eadie, and Ben each walked from the house to the road and back again, and made calculations, and then they compared notes. One hundred and ten feet, they decided. That qualified as being at least 100 feet back from the road, which was the settlement regulation.

Ben held up his metal detector. "Shall we give this a try?"

He swept the wand back and forth around the outside walls of the shed-room. They found the usual wire and nails, but they also found half a pair of scissors and a broken horseshoe. But there was no outstanding response from the metal detector that might indicate a box of gold buried nearby.

The external walls of the shed-room were clad in white brick, just like the rest of the house. It looked exactly like part of the house. They peered underneath: the foundation was built up with fieldstone. But, on further inspection, they noticed that the foundation of the whole house was fieldstone. So that didn't get them anywhere.

They decided to mark off 100 feet from the road and follow the line parallel to the road and through other people's properties looking for log cabin sites. They would sweep along the line with the metal detector, heading west toward the brow of Reservoir Hill.

It was slow work. They swept through the field around their house. It was flat and hadn't been ploughed in forever. They saw no trace of any cabin. All they turned up were some old nails.

The next field belonged to a neighbour, so they had to stop and ask Mrs. Swain for permission to go into the field and to use their metal detector. They explained that they were looking for log cabins, for a school project. *Well, who knows, we might need a project for a history fair sometime,* Eadie thought as she smiled, crossed her fingers, and told the little white lie. They didn't tell Mrs. Swain about General Procter or the Legend of the Paymaster's Gold.

It turned out, though, that there was nothing in that field other than the usual bits of metal and fencing. If there had been a cabin, it would probably have been where the Swains' front lawn was now. But the lawn had been transformed by landscapers who had brought in new topsoil and covered up whatever had been there before. If there ever had been a log cabin there, they would never find traces of it now.

They went on to the next neighbour's field. The Hanburys'. Once again, they went through the explanation of why they wanted to go into the field with a metal detector. Mr. Hanbury gave permission, so they began their long, careful sweeps.

It was Sam who bumped into the pile of rocks, overgrown with weeds. But it was Eadie who realized what it was.

"Those rocks are the same size as the ones for the foundation of our shed-room," she said. "Maybe whoever used this field after the log cabin was gone gathered all the foundation stones in one place so he could plough the rest of the field."

They swept the metal detector out in all directions from the rock pile, hoping to catch something within the ever-widening circle. At first, they found the usual things — nails and a horseshoe. Then they found a buckle, perhaps from a horse's harness. But, best of all, they found a bent and twisted spoon! Eadie was delighted. They couldn't really be exact about the site of a cabin, but it was quite easy to see that the number of finds were fewer as they went out in all directions from the rock pile.

"This has got to be a log cabin site!" Ben grinned and switched off the metal detector.

"This is so cool." Sam and Ben high-fived.

Eadie looked around the field in amazement. It wasn't just an abandoned field now: it was a settler's cabin. A settler who might have seen General Procter go by all those years ago, or heard the Kentucky Riflemen shooting their muskets at Captain Carroll! If their shed-room had been a log cabin, and this site was, too ... anything was possible. She looked west toward the next field. It was the closest to the top of Reservoir Hill and the closest to where Procter's skirmish had taken place. If there had been a cabin there, it would have been the handiest one for any paymaster wanting to hide his gold....

But Ben interrupted her thoughts. "This is it, guys. That next field is Old Tucker's place. We can't go there."

Chapter Nine

November 1813

Father and Mr. Tucker agree that the war is foolish. Nobody is winning and everyone is starving. There were fires west of here last night. American raiders were burning settlers' barns. Father spent all day digging pits in the woods to hide our grain. And Mother and I went back and forth carrying sacks of grain to bury. We cannot let the Americans steal our grain. Father does not know what to do about the cows. The Americans steal cattle as well as grain. We could walk them deep into the woods, away from the road and away from the American raiders, but then bears might attack them.

The builders came to begin work on the shed-room the next day. John was the boss and his son, Brad, was his mate. They stood in blue jeans and work boots, side by side, staring at the floor where Sam and Eadie had stripped back the layers of old linoleum, revealing wood underneath.

"That's some old floor," John said. He took off his baseball cap and scratched his grey head thoughtfully. "How old is this house?"

"The woman Mum and Dad bought it from, Mrs. Foster, said that it was built in 1865," Eadie said.

"I'm surprised to see floorboards as wide as these in a house built as late as 1865. You need very old trees from the primeval forest to get planks as wide as these."

"They're as wide as the logs you see in log cabins," Brad said. He knelt down to look at them more closely.

Eadie caught her breath. *Maybe, just maybe, the shed-room is from earlier than 1865!*

Liz turned to the twins. "Since the builders are starting today, I want you to keep out of their way and not bother them. I'd like you to do outside work for me. The lawn needs mowing and the flower bed needs weeding. There's lots to do."

"But, Mum," they protested in unison. "Ben's coming over."

"He can help, and stay for the day. We'll have a barbecue and hamburgers for supper. You can make some brownies if you like, this afternoon."

Silence.

"Anyway, I want you to stick around home today in case the builders need anything. But they know that they can call me at work if they need to. I'm late. Got to go." And she dashed out the door.

Ben came soon after. He pitched in to help Sam and Eadie dig over the flower bed and mow the lawn. After a while, Eadie stopped weeding and got up from her knees.

She wiped her dirty hands on her shorts."You know our shed-room, Ben, with its wide-plank floorboards?"

Ben nodded.

"The builders think the planks are as wide as you would find in log cabins!"

Ben grinned. "This is getting better and better!"

"Exactly. Mum told the builders that she wanted them to break through the wall of the shed-room into the kitchen because she wants a door there. I can't wait to see what the builders find when they cut the hole!"

Sam kept going around to the back of the house to peek in at John and Brad. "They're awfully slow," he complained.

Just before lunch, they heard a shout. They dashed around to the shed-room to see what was up.

"You've got a surprise here." John grinned. "Take a look at this."

He had rigged up a light to see by since there were no windows in the shed-room. He and Brad had pulled off the rough plaster on the wall so they could break through into the kitchen.

"It's logs!" Sam and Eadie and Ben exclaimed together. "The wall is made of logs!"

"It's my log cabin," shouted Eadie.

Sam and Ben whooped and shouted.

John and Brad laughed. "We've come across this kind of thing before. A log cabin inside a bigger house. I guess that when people could afford to build themselves a proper house, it made sense to keep the old cabin for storage or whatever."

"But when do you think the log cabin was built?" Eadie asked anxiously.

"I couldn't tell you that. You say the house was built in 1865? Who knows how old the log cabin was by then."

"Do you think it was built by 1812?" Sam blurted out.

"I'm no good at history." John laughed. "You'll have to look that up in the books. But this road, Commissioners Road, was here then, you know. Have you ever heard about the Legend of the Paymaster's Gold?"

Ben laughed.

Sam groaned.

But Eadie smiled politely. She was willing to listen to John's version of the legend. Maybe she would hear something new, some detail she hadn't heard before. "What's that all about?"

John leaned back against the log wall and crossed his arms against his chest. He thought for a moment. "It was the War of 1812. You know, when Canada and the United States fought each other. The British soldiers were here, to defend us. A general, Procter was his name, was escaping from the Americans and he came by here, on Commissioners Road, on his way east toward Lake Ontario, along with his soldiers. The Americans caught up with him, right here on the hill, you know, the hairpin bend, and there was a scuffle. Anyway, the Americans went off and Procter went on his way. But somewhere in the skirmish his gold went missing. They say that the gold was to pay his soldiers."

Sam and Ben both spoke at the same time.

"How much gold?"

"Did anyone ever find it?"

John picked up his lunch box from the floor and headed outside for a bit of fresh air. Sam and Eadie and Ben followed him. "A lot of gold, I suppose. I don't think it was ever found because people still tell the story. I heard it when I was a kid. Everybody who grew up around here has heard it."

John sat down on the woodpile and opened his lunch box. Brad sat down beside him. But Eadie had one more question.

"Do you think the gold was truly lost, in a field or something, or do you think it was hidden away for safe keeping?"

"Well, then. We won't know that until it's found." And John turned his attention to his sandwich.

Sam, Eadie, and Ben went back into the shed-room. It was amazing to look at the wall of logs. Eadie placed her hand on the logs and felt their angled surfaces. They had been roughly squared. She could see marks from the adze that had shaped them. She counted. "Five logs high. That's not many. Look at the size of them. They're huge! Who'd have thought ... we thought that this shed-room was strange, but this is amazing!"

Ben suggested that his dad could take a tree core from the logs. That wouldn't tell them when the log cabin was built, of course, but it would tell them how old the huge trees were at the time that they were cut. And that would be interesting to know.

They were interrupted by John. He came inside, pulled a scrap of paper out of his pocket, and gave it to Eadie. "You're keen on mysteries," he said, "maybe this is a clue. We found it stuck to a bit of the plaster off the wall. It's the only piece we found, but it has writing on it." He smiled and went outside again to finish his lunch.

"What is it, Eadie?" Ben asked.

"It's got writing on it, old-fashioned writing. It's hard to make out." She turned and went outside where the light was better. The boys followed.

"Oh," she smiled. "I've read about this in books. Look. Whoever wrote it, wrote down the page and then turned the page and wrote across the first writing!"

"What a stupid thing to do!" Sam said. "Now you can hardly read it."

"It was to save paper. If this was written during the War of 1812, so early in the settlement here, then paper would have been scarce."

"Do you think that it's that old?" Ben asked.

"What does it say?" Sam was impatient.

"I can make out, 'killed at Queenston' and 'battle fought.'" Eadie turned the paper to read the writing in the other direction, "'Hide in cellar,' and 'silver spoons.'"

"Brock was killed at Queenston!"

"And the battle must refer to the War of 1812!"

"Did someone hide spoons in a cellar?"

"A cellar? It could it be our cellar! This must have been a cabin in 1812!"

Ben said, "*If* the shed-room really was a log cabin...."

Eadie interrupted, "And *if* it really was here in 1812...."

Sam added, "And *if* someone hid silver spoons in it, then maybe they're still here!"

Ben stood still and looked at Sam and Eadie. "Then the cellar in this log cabin would have been a super hiding place for the paymaster's gold, too!"

Eadie looked at the torn and dirty scrap of paper again. She asked, "Who'd you think wrote this?" But the boys weren't listening. They were figuring out how to get into the cellar which Sam and Eadie's dad had declared to be out of bounds.

The squiggly letters sloped across the yellowed paper." This must have been written right here, during the war," Eadie said to herself, "by someone who was living here, in our shed-room! Except — it was a log cabin then."

It was only a scrap of yellowed paper but it made the war come alive for Eadie: soldiers marching on the road, American raiders riding through, threatening families, stealing livestock, setting fire to barns. She shivered. "Sam and Ben just think that the war would have been exciting, but I think it would have been more scary than exciting."

Eadie put the paper carefully into her pocket. She turned to listen to the boys.

"We've got to get inside that cellar, by ourselves, to have a better look around," Sam was saying. "We never really got a decent look when we went down into it with Dad. He wouldn't let us touch anything...."

"But your parents told you not to go down into the cellar."

Sam ran his fingers through his hair in frustration.

"Old Tucker won't let us on his land to look for log cabin sites. And Mum and Dad won't let us go down into the cellar here when we know that this is a log cabin...."

"Which was here as early as the War of 1812, for sure!" Eadie added.

Ben sighed. "What good is a metal detector if you can't get into the best places to use it?"

Chapter Ten

January 1814

Freezing cold. Too cold for the cows. We had to pack straw around their shed to keep them warm. We have to keep them alive. It is too cold for war. Everything is quiet just now. John even came home for a few days at Christmas. That was the best present! He was half-starved and terribly thin. He told us about a lady called Laura Secord who walked through the night last summer to take a message to Lieutenant FitzGibbon and the British soldiers that the Americans were coming. There was a battle and he was so brave that he was promoted to Captain. Laura Secord must have been brave, too, like Phoebe McNames.

After lunch, Sam and Ben settled down at the computer to search the Internet. They wanted to know how to build an abatis.

"Tell me again, what's an abatis?" asked Eadie.

Sam explained, "Remember? It's for defence. Here, this website says that you cut brushwood to build it up like a wall with the tips pointing outwards against the enemy. Like a bristles on a brush. You can hide behind it when you're firing your musket."

"It's what General Procter didn't build at Moraviantown," Ben added. Dave at the library had told them that he was involved with a military re-enactment society. He said that he might find a place for them in a re-enactment in the fall. They would have to help make an abatis.

Eadie left them to it. She had a plan of her own. She wanted to find out more about Phoebe McNames. Dave had told her that there were McNames gravestones in Brick Street Cemetery. She got on her bike and headed east along Commissioners Road. The cemetery was not far away, just a few kilometres.

Eadie had heard about Laura Secord in her history classes. Laura Secord was famous for helping the soldiers in the War of 1812 by walking all night through the bush to warn Lieutenant FitzGibbon about plans for an American invasion that she'd overheard. Eadie couldn't understand why Phoebe McNames wasn't famous. She had helped the soldiers, too, by passing them their ammunition during Procter's skirmish on Reservoir Hill.

I guess Phoebe can't be famous if that skirmish is only a legend and didn't really happen. Eadie sighed. She could imagine Phoebe dashing from her log cabin, somewhere along Commissioners Road, taking buckets of water for the soldiers to drink and helping them load their muskets. Why did she do it? Maybe her husband was away at the war and she was alone. Maybe it was a way of seeking protection from the British soldiers? Would loyal Phoebe have offered a hiding place for the paymaster's gold? If she did, was the gold reclaimed afterward, or not? Did Phoebe McNames live in their shed-room when it was a log cabin?

Eadie found the cemetery easily. There was a metal sign. Eadie paused to read it.

> BRICK STREET CEMETERY
>
> This cemetery served as the burial ground for settlers who first arrived in Westminster Township, 1810. In use by 1819, it is situated on land originally granted to Peter McNames and James Sheldon. Though the farms which once surrounded it have been subdivided, the Brick Street Cemetery, now the charge of the Mount Zion United Church, remains as a memorial to our pioneer ancestors.

Eadie felt a shiver of emotion. She felt so close to the past. So close to the people who had lived on Commissioners Road before her. *Imagine,* she thought, *the first settlers only came around the time of the War of 1812. And they needed a cemetery so soon, 1819. I suppose some of those burials were babies. You always read in history books that lots of children died young, long ago.*

The cemetery had rows and rows of tombstones, many of them very old. Just simple, thin, white stones, rounded at the top. Eadie wandered up and down the rows, ignoring the bigger, more expensive, and more recent tombstones.

She was looking for older ones. Suddenly she saw it: not an upright stone, but a flat one, broken, lying in the grass. She could just make out, "Phoebe, wife of ... McNames" and then, on the broken bit, "Peter." *Maybe he was Phoebe's husband?* Eadie stared at the tombstone for a long time, trying to imagine what sort of person Phoebe had been. *Brave, for sure. And loyal. And strong, too.*

Eadie reached into her knapsack for her notebook where she had jotted down notes from her dad's historical atlas. Eadie read out loud to Phoebe McNames's tombstone. It was Eadie's way of honouring Phoebe.

> To the record of this gallant exploit must be added a brief mention of the heroic conduct of a woman, Mrs. McNames.... Her husband was away on duty as a militiaman, and when the fight began near her house she sprang upon a baggage wagon and, regardless of the bullets which whistled around her, she handed out ammunition to the troops and carried water for them to drink during the whole of the engagement. A country inhabited, as Canada was, by a people as brave and as loyal as Mrs. McNames, although it might be overrun by a hostile army for a season ... could not be conquered....

"There you are, Phoebe. Someone long ago believed that this really happened and I think so, too." Eadie closed her notebook. In her mind's eye, she could see the whole scene. Procter dashing on ahead, Carroll's men frantically trying to get the baggage wagons up Reservoir Hill, others clawing their way up the sides of the ravine to shoot down on the Kentucky Riflemen, and Mrs. McNames dashing to help them, her long skirt becoming streaked with dirt, her hair falling loose and blowing in the wind.

Eadie wandered on among the tombstones. Then she saw other McNames tombstones, which was confusing. There was a stone to the memory of Peter McNames. And one to a daughter of Peter and Phoebe. How many Peter McNameses were there? And how many Phoebes? Sons named after fathers. Daughters named after mothers. Whatever the truth was, Eadie decided to believe that a Phoebe McNames was indeed a heroine of the War of 1812. *It's a shame,* Eadie thought, *that no one talks about Phoebe McNames.*

Eadie sat on a bench near Phoebe's grave to review what she knew about the paymaster and his gold. There really had been settlers living there at the time of the War of 1812. All of them would have built log houses. If there had been a paymaster with Captain Carroll's group of militia, what had he done with his gold during the skirmish on Reservoir Hill? Did he hide it with a settler family? Then, where was it now? Had the paymaster been killed in the skirmish? Had the Americans raided the log house where it was hidden and taken it away? *How can I find out the truth? And what is the truth? Legends! They're so complicated! What do I believe?*

Eadie thought of the story that had been told through the generations in her mother's family. It was about Great-Great-Great-Grandmother Murray. She was a pioneer, a settler, all those years ago in the early 1800s. The story was that she walked twenty miles through the bush — in fact, all through the night through the bush — to get to the gristmill. She carried a sack of grain with her to get ground into flour.

Remembering this story, Eadie smiled to herself and her eyes got what Sam called her "dreamy look." It was one of her favourite stories. She could imagine her great-great-great-grandmother making her way through the forest, bent over, carrying her sack of grain, but determined to get it made into flour for her family. Eadie thought of wolves and bears and nighttime in the forest, and shivered. Grandma Murray should have won a bravery award.

But, when Eadie asked if the story was true, her mother had said, "We have no documents from the miller, no receipts. And Grandma Murray didn't keep a diary or write that incident down...."

So it was only a legend. A lot of families with pioneer histories told the same story about their grandmothers. Some of the stories could be true, though. There were only scattered pioneer homes, and the early gristmills were few and far apart. But whether the grandmothers really walked twenty miles through the bush to get to the mill may or may not have happened.

Eadie took out her camera and photographed Phoebe's grave. Then she climbed on her bike and made her way slowly home.

Sam and Ben had left a note: "Come to our woods." So Eadie walked out behind the house, past the old apple orchard to the little woods. She couldn't see the boys anywhere until they jumped up and shouted. They had been hiding behind a wall of brushwood.

"We've made an abatis, Eadie!"

"Just like the soldiers did in the War of 1812."

"See? It's just dragging tree limbs together so that the branches face outward. We can hide behind it," Sam said.

"Pretend you're the enemy and try to get through."

Eadie tried. "You're right. It's hard to shift because all the boughs are tangled together. And it's prickly. Although," she paused, "maybe if I had on a woollen uniform I wouldn't feel the sharp pointy bits...."

"Well, yes, it should have some bigger limbs of trees in it, but Dad would get mad if we really hacked the bushes to death."

Eadie looked at the abatis more closely. "It's great. How long did it take you to make it?"

"About two hours. But there's only Ben and me. If we were a company of thirty militia, not a problem. We could do it really fast."

"You've cut down a lot of brush, Sam...."

"It's research, Eadie."

"For Dave," Ben added.

"Is that what Dave wants you to build at the re-enactment?"

"Yeah. We're going to ask him to come and see this one, to see if it's all right."

The boys didn't ask about Eadie's afternoon and she never told them. It was private, between Phoebe McNames and herself.

Chapter Eleven

March 1814

The weather is warmer. Snow's almost gone. Father is worried that the American raids will begin again. I visited Lucy today because the Tuckers were making maple sugar. She showed me all the wool she has spun this winter. A lot more than me. And it's finer, too. Mine is all knobbly. Mother says that it will do to knit into a blanket. Mrs. Tucker showed me her big china bowl, all white with fancy writing and coloured flowers painted on it. It has two handles. The writing says "Elizabeth and James Tucker, Dymock, Glos, 1809." Their friends gave it to them when they left England. I am going to show Lucy our six silver spoons. Mother kept them tucked in her dress all the time we were travelling here. One spoon is very special. It is a marriage spoon made for Father and Mother. It was made in England, before they came to America. It was made by a lady silversmith in London called Hester Bateman. "Hester Bateman." That's a lovely name. It says "HB" on the back of the spoon. The front of it is all decorated with rows of tiny marks and initials A and R W. Annie and Robert Wareham. My name is the same as Mother's.

The next day, the telephone woke Eadie up. It was John, the builder. He said that he wouldn't be coming. He and his son, Brad, had to go to a funeral. Eadie said sympathetic things, like she had heard her parents say on such occasions. "Sorry about that, John. See you later. When you're ready."

She looked at her watch: 9:00 a.m. Her parents had both gone to work. She pounded on Sam's door. "Get up, Sam, this is our big chance!"

"Chance for what?"

"To get into the cellar!"

While Sam got up, Eadie phoned Ben to come right over and to bring his metal detector.

Breakfast forgotten, Eadie found two flashlights in the kitchen and three shovels in the garage. When Sam came downstairs, she got him to help to bring a ladder in from the garage. Everything was ready when Ben arrived.

Sam and Eadie explained to Ben that the builder wasn't coming.

"But your parents said —"

"Yes, we know," Sam interrupted. "But this is gold, Ben. Gold! They won't be mad at us if we find the gold. We know our shed-room is a pioneer cabin now."

"And that someone hid silver spoons in the cellar," Eadie added.

Ben shrugged and picked up his metal detector. "It's on your head."

"Here we go." Sam lifted the trap door.

Sam went down into the cellar first. Eadie and Ben passed him the shovels. Then Eadie went down. Ben went down the ladder last, with his metal detector.

The cellar was cool and dark and damp. They paused to listen. Rustling noises? Mice?

"This is spooky." Ben hadn't been down in the cellar before.

"We've got to look everywhere," Sam said. "That's why we need the shovels. We've got to poke into the corners, and maybe even scrape the floor a little, in case some earth from the walls has fallen down in the last two hundred years."

The twins turned and looked at Ben. They waited.

Ben switched on the metal detector.

Nothing. Not a peep.

They couldn't believe it.

"Well," Sam said, "we haven't really poked around yet. Let's dig a little."

Cautiously, they began to feel their way around the cellar. Eadie held the flashlights while Ben swept his metal detector back and forth across the cellar floor. They explored the cellar more thoroughly than their father had. They walked into curtains of spider webs and stirred up years of dust with every step.

Nothing.

"Do you think the batteries are dead?" Sam asked hopefully.

"Nope. I checked them before I came over."

"Let's climb up the ladder and poke in beside all those beams in the ceiling," Eadie suggested. "Maybe they didn't hide anything in a box in the ground. Maybe they hid coins, scattered them around, under the beams. Or, maybe the silver spoons."

They went back and forth, checking for anything tucked in beside the beams, sweeping the floor methodically with the metal detector. Nothing.

"Let's dig," said Eadie. "Like archaeologists! A hole in each corner and one in the middle. If there's anything here, it'll be close enough for the metal detector to beep."

Again, Eadie held the flashlights while the boys dug holes. Even though the cellar was cool, they were sweating. But their shovels felt nothing hard, like a paymaster's box. And the metal detector was silent.

"Not even a rusty, old nail," Sam said. He threw down his shovel in disgust.

"I can't believe it," Eadie said, staring at the holes. "We know this shed-room was a log cabin. I was convinced that it was here in 1812. I thought we might find more scraps of paper with writing, too. And what about the silver spoons?"

"I guess that was wishful thinking, Eadie." Ben switched the metal detector off.

The boys filled in the holes and smoothed everything down so that their parents would never know that they'd been down in the cellar. Then they brought up the ladder and the shovels and put them away. After everything was tidied up, they made some breakfast. Pancakes with lots of butter and maple syrup to make themselves feel better. Usually, they tried to eat their age in pancakes, but not today. They didn't have the heart for it.

"Where else can we look?" Sam asked, his chin in his hands. He pushed his pancakes away and slumped down in his chair. "Maybe it's only a legend after all."

Eadie thought of Phoebe McNames. She had never made it into the history books, like Laura Secord had, so maybe the skirmish never happened. Maybe Phoebe was never called upon to help the soldiers. She sighed. Maybe there was no gold.

Silence.

Each of them was lost in thought. It had seemed like such a good idea. After all, when a skirmish happened on your doorstep, then gold had gone missing, how could you not search for it?

Suddenly, Ben sat up and thumped the table. The plates jumped. Sam and Eadie looked at him. "The only place we haven't looked is Old Tucker's place."

"But his dogs!" Eadie protested.

"He'd tell our parents if he caught us on his land," Sam said. "They'd be so mad."

"I've got an idea," said Ben.

Chapter Twelve

June 1814

The government wants everyone to work harder on the road building. Father and Mr. Tucker and all the men have been hauling gravel all day. They found some good gravel on Mr. Tucker's land. The government will pay him for it. I don't understand. If the road is made better, our soldiers will be better able to travel on it — but, so will the Americans when they come to raid us! We have had no word from John in Niagara for months now.

"Old Tucker won't let us on his land," Ben said. "But we could sneak into the gravel company's property on the far side of Tucker's field."

"The company has a no trespassing sign up," Sam said gloomily.

"I know that. But that's because they don't want anyone getting chewed up in their machinery. In that corner near Old

Tucker's field, they don't even have a road up there or any trucks. We could stay right along the fenceline and we'd be okay. If worse came to worse, they'd just tell us to get out."

"So, how is going along Old Tucker's fenceline by the gravel pit going to help us?" Eadie asked, toying with her pancakes.

"Think about it. Where's your map of the settlement pattern, Eadie?" Eadie found it in her knapsack. Ben took it and grabbed a pencil from the kitchen counter. He pushed the sticky plates out of the way and flattened out Eadie's map on the kitchen table.

"Look, here's your house, 100 feet back from the road. And here's the Swains' house, a little farther back from the road. That's probably because it's not an old house. And west of them is the Hanburys' house and the field where we found the pile of rocks that we think was the foundation of a cabin. That was also about 100 feet from the road." He drew the rock pile on Eadie's map.

"But we can look at this a different way. Eadie's idea was to measure the 100 feet in from Commissioners Road. But we can measure something else, too. Look how far apart each of the houses is to the next one. See? Your house, the Swains', and the Hanburys' are all more or less the same distance from each other, one on each property." Ben drew lines on the map to measure the distance between the houses. "Except for Old Tucker. His house is not so old. You can see that by looking at it. So, if we go along the same distance again, west from Hanburys', we get to Old Tucker's fenceline."

"Who would build a log cabin on the fenceline?" Sam asked.

"No one," Ben said patiently. "I think that Old Tucker sold some land to the gravel company. And moved the fence."

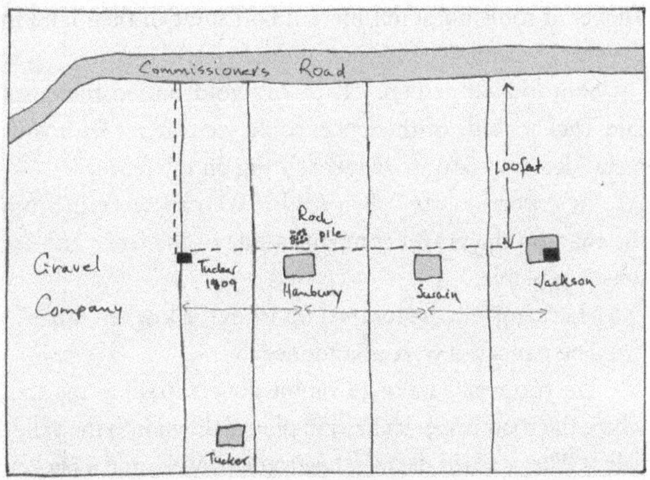

Eadie looked at what Ben had drawn on her map. It made sense. A row of log cabins equal distance, 100 feet or so; from the road and more or less an equal distance from each other. The first organized settlement, each family on their assigned lot of land, houses built according to the government's rules of settlement. Just like the patterns she had seen on the maps Dave had shown her in the library. The house Old Tucker lived in now was not so old and it was about 200 feet back from the road. In fact, they could see that his property was not as wide as Jacksons', Swains', and Hanburys' properties.

"Okay," Sam said, getting his head around what Ben had said and studying the map. "We know that the distance from our house to Swains' and from Swains' to Hanbury's rock pile is more or less the same. So, the same distance again, westward, should give us the site of the original Tucker log cabin."

"Exactly!" Ben grinned. "And it would be on the fenceline, not in the centre of his property, because some

Tucker at some point in time, sold off some of their land to the gravel company and moved the fence."

Sam looked at Ben. "If there's gold buried there, on Old Tucker's side of the fence, could we reach it with your metal detector. Say, if we were sitting on the fence?"

"It's worth a try," Ben said. "We can walk in from the road on the gravel company's side of the fence and see what's possible."

"Let's go!" Eadie jumped up from the kitchen table.

The pancakes were abandoned.

The trio walked along Commissioners Road to the spot where the road began its hairpin plunge down into the valley below. They carried the metal detector, trowels, and a bucket. They then walked in from the road along the fenceline, keeping on the gravel company's side of it. They each counted their paces and agreed with each other when they got 100 feet in from the road. If there was a log cabin, it would be here, or a little farther than the 100 feet along the fenceline.

Ben switched on the metal detector. Nothing. They began the methodical sweep on their side of the fence, walking in, farther from the road. Eadie counted their paces. At about 118 feet, they heard a beep. Experienced by now, they didn't get too excited. And sure enough, it was a nail. But a nail was good. A nail in the middle of a field meant that there might have been a house there at one time. In another few steps they found another nail, and then a horseshoe, and then a spike.

"Okay," Ben said. "Now we need to double back, a little farther out from the fence. Here, on the gravel company's side of the fence."

They did this, sweeping back across a 16-foot patch, which they estimated might be the cabin site. But all they found was a bit of fence wire.

"Right," Eadie said. "Most of the log cabin site, if it is one, must lie more on Tucker's side of the fence." She looked at Ben, then at Sam.

The boys looked over the fence to Tucker's field. Fear of Old Tucker was swiftly forgotten. The lure of gold was too strong.

"Let's go!" Ben shouted.

"Old Tucker won't mind us on his land if we find him some gold!"

The boys clambered over the fence with the metal detector, trowels, and bucket.

"Eadie, climb the tree and keep a look out for Old Tucker," Sam ordered.

Sam and Ben began searching next to the fence, across the 16-foot patch where they figured the log cabin might have been. The metal detector suddenly erupted into beeps. More nails and bits of harness. When they dug, the boys also found broken bits of china — small pieces of white and blue and green that must have been someone's dishes once, long ago. They handed them up to Eadie in the tree.

Eadie loved to find these broken bits. They made her feel connected to whoever had lived there before. She was especially excited when she came across several pieces that had words painted on them. She made out "Dym" on one piece and "1809" on another one.

"I wish that I could find enough pieces to stick them all together to make a pot, like archaeologists do," she called down to the boys as she put the pieces carefully in her knapsack.

Sam and Ben were not interested in broken pottery. They dug in any spot where they got the slightest beep from the metal detector. They were looking for gold!

Next, the boys dug up a spoon. Twisted and dirty, but a spoon nonetheless. Eadie climbed down from the tree to have a closer look at it. She took out her camera and photographed it, front and back.

On the front, on the handle, was a very pretty pattern of marks and letters engraved: "A R and W." On the back of the spoon were stamped the letters "HB." *These marks,* Eadie thought. *What are they called? Hallmarks? Maker's mark? Whatever, I can look these up on the Web and find out how old the spoon is!* Eadie was so absorbed in looking at the spoon that she forgot to keep an eye out for Old Tucker.

All of a sudden, there was an eruption of barking. Eadie looked up and saw Old Tucker's dogs streaking down the grassy field. They dropped everything — the metal detector and spades — and ran for the fence. They made it over and up the tree just in the nick of time. The dogs were in a frenzy. Barking and snarling and jumping up at the fence. Then they saw Old Tucker.

"I told you not to come on my land!" He shouted after them.

Ben had left the metal detector on Old Tucker's side of the fence. He couldn't go home without it. His dad would never forgive him. Trespassing, too. Sam, Eadie, and Ben scrambled from the fence, higher up into the tree. They waited for Old Tucker to give them an earful.

Which he did.

Old Tucker told the dogs to shut up, then he laid in to Sam, Ben, and Eadie. He was especially hard on Ben, whom he recognized. Old Tucker stood there, short and angry, in his faded overalls and greasy, floppy hat. His teeth were rotten, his hands were dirty. He couldn't stand trespassers, he said. "Especially city folk." He glowered at them. They listened in silence.

But when he paused to think of something else to say, Eadie spoke up.

"Mr. Tucker," she said boldly, "you haven't asked us why we're searching your field with a metal detector."

Old Tucker scowled. "Well? Why are you?"

Eadie gave him her sweetest smile. "We're searching for gold. Lost gold. The Paymaster's Gold. You must know the legend, Mr. Tucker."

Old Tucker hesitated. He crossed his tanned and muscled arms across his barrel chest and glared at Eadie. "Of course I know the Legend of the Paymaster's Gold. Everyone who grew up around here knows it."

Eadie was encouraged. She just might talk him around. "We figured out that this might have been the site of a settler's cabin, 100 feet from the road, and if the cabin was here in 1813, the paymaster might have hidden the gold here."

"I could've told you that the log cabin was here, if you'd asked me," Old Tucker grumped. He stood a little straighter and spoke proudly. "It's only Tuckers have ever been on this land. Right from the beginning of settlement."

"When was that?"asked Sam.

"Tuckers settled here in 1809 and filed for our grant in 1829. We've still got that paper. We're one of the first settlers in this whole area."

Sam and Eadie and Ben gave a whoop.

"1809! Perfect!" Eadie felt goosebumps of excitement.

"We've got it!" Sam punched Ben in glee.

"Awesome!" Ben couldn't believe it.

"Now see here—"Old Tucker began.

But Eadie smiled again. "If you let us check this cabin site with our metal detector, Mr. Tucker, we might find the gold. See, we've already found a silver spoon."

Eadie leaned down from the tree and held it out to him. He took it with a look of amazement. "Well, I never." He held it in the palm of his grimy hand and turned it over and over.

"Do you know anything about the spoon?" Eadie asked. "Is there any family history about it? As far as I can make out, the initials on it are *A, R,* and *W.*"

"I don't rightly know about the dates, but there was an Annie Wareham who married into the Tuckers early on. Maybe it's connected with her."

Eadie wanted to keep Old Tucker talking. "Where did the Tuckers come from?"

"England. Some place called Dimmock."

Sam was becoming impatient with all this chatter.

"We're looking for the gold, Mr. Tucker," Sam reminded him.

Old Tucker looked up sharply. "So you think you'll find the gold here?"

"Yes," Sam said. But he was worried that if they found the gold on Old Tucker's land, Old Tucker would claim it all for himself. After all their work. He had to think quickly.

"But if it's the paymaster's gold, Mr. Tucker, then we get to split it. Finders Keepers. Half to you because it's on your land. And half to us because we found it."

Eadie and Ben held their breath. Then Eadie saw a small smile play at the corner of Old Tucker's mouth and a twinkle in his eye.

"I see," he said gruffly, "that's the deal, is it?"

Sam held his nerve, "Yes, sir. That's the deal. Fifty-fifty."

There was a long silence while Old Tucker looked first at Sam, then at the metal detector, and, finally, at the silver spoon in his hand. Then he raised his eyes, looked at Sam, and said, "Fair enough then. Get on with it."

"Thank you!" The trio chimed in unison.

"And, please, Mr. Tucker, can you call off your dogs?" Ben added.

Chapter Thirteen

August 31, 1814

Terrible news! There was a skirmish on the big hill last night and Captain Carroll was killed! War is so cruel. The captain was so handsome and brave and kind. We are all upset and Lucy and I cannot stop crying. It was that horrible Andrew Westbrook who led seventy American Rangers in a raid to Oxford, east of here. They were stealing cattle and money and captured Captain Carroll. Captain Rapelje organized our militia and ambushed the Americans on the hill. We heard the guns! The wounded were brought to Tuckers' and to us, so we were up all night. Andrew Westbrook and the Americans escaped into the woods. He will come back and raid the settlers again. Today Lucy and I are going to search on the hill to see if Westbrook's men dropped anything — like pouches of ammunition or purses of stolen money. I wish the war was over. I am tired of being frightened.

Old Tucker didn't hang around to watch them work. He called his dogs and strode off across the field toward his house.

"Hey, Sam, good work!" Ben said."We've got a deal! And Eadie, too. You really turned Old Tucker around!"

Eadie smiled.

Once again, they set to work. They paced out the boundaries of the 16-by-20-foot cabin site, at least, as far as they were able to estimate it. Then they began the slow and methodical search with the metal detector. They were kept very busy. Lots of metal bits and another spoon. Then three soldier's buttons! That gave them hope. A buckle from a harness, an old cooking pot, and two rusty door hinges came next. It was a lot of digging. Every moment of excitement when they got a response from the metal detector was followed by a blow of disappointment when they dug and didn't find gold.

Only Eadie got pleasure from the hunt. She loved finding all the leftover bits of a household long gone: pieces of broken china, a tiny medicine bottle of dark brown glass, handmade nails, a buckle, three buttons made of pottery. Eadie had visited pioneer museums, and this was like bringing a museum to life. She could imagine the log cabin in her mind's eye, right down to the roughly made furniture. Nothing fancy, a bench or two, a solid wooden table. The mother of the house thumping bread dough and stirring a stew pot over the fire on the hearth. Eadie thought of the two spoons they had found. So precious, probably brought from England. A treasure, a keepsake. A memory of home.

They were hot and tired and dirty and hungry. They took a break and ate all the energy bars that Eadie had in her knapsack. Ben smeared himself with sunscreen again. But they couldn't stop. Old Tucker's site was their last hope of finding the gold. They had to keep at it. What if Old Tucker changed his mind and came back and chased them off his property?

They had completed sweeping across the whole width of the cabin site except for one corner. By now they were feeling a little dejected. Doubts had begun to creep in. They had felt so good about finding the cabin site. It had seemed such a sure way to find the gold. And Old Tucker had confirmed that the cabin had been built in 1809.

Then why couldn't they find the gold?

Ben was just about to suggest that they leave it for another day and go find something to eat besides power bars when the metal detector reacted. Loud and clear. More so than anywhere else on the site. They looked at each other hopefully. Ben threw down the metal detector and he and Eadie helped Sam dig.

It was buried quite deep. They felt their trowels hit against something that resisted. It was pieces of wood, soft and rotten. And then they heard a chinking sound. Metal!

"Careful!" Ben said. "Maybe the box has rotted away." They abandoned the trowels and began to dig with their hands, running their fingers through the earth. Every handful yielded a reward.

Coins! Some big. Some small. But they were dirty and dull. Eadie picked up an old plastic container — modern rubbish, blown against the fence — and poured her bottled water into it. She dipped the coins into the water to wash the soil away.

It was magic.

"Gold!"

"Look at that!"

"I can't believe this is happening!"

Some of the coins shone brightly. Others remained dull. Silver? Copper? Some were big and some were small. Some appeared to be English but others seemed more foreign.

"Is this the paymaster's gold, do you think?" Ben asked anxiously.

"The box has rotted away. It's hard to tell if it's an official paymaster's box," Sam said.

"What else can it be?" Eadie asked. "It fits. We're here, right at the cabin nearest where the skirmish was."

The boys continued to sift through the earth for coins. Eadie took out her camera and photographed the site and the boys digging and the coins laid out on an old piece of plastic bag. "We've got to record the discovery!"

When the boys realized that Eadie wasn't in any of the pictures they took some pictures of her with the spoons and pacing the perimeter of the 16-by-20-foot cabin site.

Finally, after a lot of sifting through the soil with their fingers, they found fewer and fewer coins.

"That's it," Sam said. "It looks as though we've got them all."

Ben did a final sweep with the metal detector. It was quiet.

"We've got to get these home," Sam said, sitting back on his heels. "We should hide them until we can clean them and figure out what they are."

The bucket was too small, so Sam and Ben took off their T-shirts and wrapped the extra coins in them. The coins were very heavy. Eadie slathered Ben's back with sunscreen so he wouldn't get burned.

They were exhausted and starving, but triumphant. They laughed and whooped all the way home. They just couldn't believe it.

"Ben, if you hadn't had a metal detector!"

"Eadie, if you hadn't found out about the four conditions of settlement!"

"Sam, if you hadn't stood up to Old Tucker!"

They decided not to tell Old Tucker or their parents anything. Not yet. They wanted to gloat over the coins first, enjoy the fact that they'd actually found them. And find out what they were worth. They'd tell Old Tucker tomorrow when they knew more about the coins.

The trio walked back up Commissioners Road, lugging the dead weight of the coins, and didn't complain a bit!

"Let's hide the coins in the root cellar," Eadie suggested.

"But what if John and Brad come again tomorrow," argued Sam.

"We can't let the coins out of our sight," Ben said very firmly.

"Okay," Sam shifted the weight of his T-shirt-bag of coins. "We'll have to hide them in my bedroom."

"Yeah!" Eadie agreed. "You never allow anyone into your bedroom anyway. Mum definitely won't go in there." She paused. "Oh, no! Mum is on a decorating rampage now, checking out all the rooms: which need papering, plastering, painting. She just barges in!"

Ben looked a little anxious. Then he had an idea. "What about the abatis?"

Sam and Eadie turned to him.

"Brilliant!"

"Cool!"

"We could sleep out there tonight," Ben suggested.

"Just for fun," Sam agreed.

"And to guard the gold!"

That night, the trio slept behind the abatis. In a tent.

They even dug a hole to bury the gold. Ben dragged his sleeping bag across the hole and slept on top of it. "No one's going to steal this gold!"

Settled in the tent, they decided to look up the price of gold. Sam had remembered to bring his iPhone with him to the tent. He switched it on. The battery icon flickered and died. He threw it down on his sleeping bag in frustration. "The battery's dead!"

"Sam!"

They couldn't believe it. They were dying with curiosity to know the value of the coins.

"We can't go inside the house, Sam. Mum and Dad will only ask questions." Eadie reached into her knapsack and pulled out a section from yesterday's newspaper. "Look, guys. Here's the closing prices for commodities."

Ben laughed. "Eadie wins again!"

They focused their flashlights on the newspaper.

"Wow! Gold is $963.55 a troy ounce!"

"But what's a troy ounce?" Ben asked.

"Well, a normal pound is 16 ounces, at least in cooking recipes," Eadie answered. "But I don't know how much a troy ounce is." She glanced down the page. "Silver is $14.58 a troy ounce. That's not much. And copper is $2.73 a pound. Even less."

"The gold's the thing."

"And there's heritage value, too. Like, what will collectors pay if the coins are rare?"

"Don't forget that it's fifty-fifty with Old Tucker."

"That's a promise."

CHAPTER FOURTEEN

November 1814

The Americans came again. It was terrible! They stole money and burned everyone's place along the Thames River. Mills, barns, haystacks. Everything! We saw the fires west of here and people ran ahead to warn us. Father drove the cows into the woods and made Mother and I stay with them. He climbed the big oak tree and said he would shoot at anyone who set fire to our hay rick or cabin. We stayed in the woods until daylight. Then Father came to rescue us. In the end, he said that the raiders were so tired and drunk that they probably could not see straight. Anyway, they are gone. Thomas Greenaway came home from Niagara and he is terribly wounded. He cannot use his right arm. We have not heard from John since last Christmas. Mother is sick with worry.

The next morning, Liz Jackson peered around behind the abatis to see check on Sam, Eadie, and Ben. They were all asleep. She smiled and went off to work.

After breakfast — well, lunch, really — which consisted of waffles and maple syrup, the trio started to work. They set up in the kitchen. Eadie washed the coins in the kitchen sink and scrubbed them with a toothbrush. Sam and Ben set up the laptop on the kitchen table and Googled the coins. It quickly became confusing. They discovered that a troy ounce was one twelfth of a pound, not one sixteenth like in cooking. They realized that the value of the coin was, at the minimum, its weight of metal. But the business of rarity was harder to understand.

They were puzzled, too, because the coins were so difficult to recognize. Who were these people whose heads were on the coins? Lots of the words didn't seem to be English. They recognized some French. And guessed that some were Spanish. Why was that? When Upper Canada was a British colony?

"Dollars. Guineas. Shillings. Florins. Livres. Doubloons. Pistareens. Florins."

"This is crazy!" Sam said. "Who can help us figure it out?

"Dave! At the library. He'll know," Eadie suggested.

"We were going to ask him to come to see the abatis anyway," Ben said.

Sam phoned Dave.

He had just put his cellphone down when there was a terrific racket outside.

"It's Old Tucker's dogs!" Ben cried.

Sam looked out the window. "It's Old Tucker himself. He doesn't look too happy."

They let him in. But not the dogs.

Old Tucker was in an angry mood. "I've seen that bloody great hole you dug in my field. Where's the gold? And where's my share?"

Sam and Ben turned to Eadie and silently willed her to turn on the charm. Which she did, of course.

"Mr. Tucker, let us explain. We did find the gold in your field. We dug it up and brought it home and kept it safe for you. Look." She pointed to the pile of coins on the kitchen table.

Mr. Tucker looked. And looked. And looked. He couldn't believe the pile of coins, how shiny the gold ones were. "That's amazing! You really did find it. I never thought you would ... just kids playing detective." He pulled out a kitchen chair, sat down, took off his tattered old hat and grinned and grinned and grinned.

"We've been trying to identify them. They're from all different countries, not just England," Sam explained.

"And we're Googling to try and find out their rarity value," Ben added.

"What's Googling?" Mr. Tucker asked.

When Liz and Tom arrived home, Sam, Eadie, and Ben were still in the kitchen. The coins were in a heap on the table and Mr. Tucker was poking his stubby fingers at the keyboard of the laptop.

"Scroll down, now, Mr. Tucker." Ben was showing him how to surf the Web. "Now, choose from the menu...."

"What's going on here?" Liz asked.

"We found the gold! We found the gold!"

"We found the paymaster's gold!"

Now it was Tom and Liz's turn to be amazed. "I never

thought … it was just a legend! How did you ever…?" Liz stammered.

There was a jumble of explanations. Sam and Eadie and Ben all talked at once: "The plaque in the park … Dave at the library… the Web … Phoebe McNames's gravestone…. The settlement regulations … Ben's metal detector … the shed-room … the 1809 piece of pottery … we drew maps."

"But," Eadie said generously "we couldn't have done it without Mr. Tucker. He gave us permission to dig up his field."

"Is that where you found it?" Tom's mind was jumbled in confusion. He was thinking, *Mr. Tucker? That cantankerous neighbour? And he's here, sitting in our kitchen, happy as a lamb. That must mean that it's Mr. Tucker's gold. It was found on his property.*

Sam spoke quickly before his parents started asking any more questions. "We have a deal with Mr. Tucker, Dad. Fifty-fifty." He turned to Mr. Tucker. "Right?"

Mr. Tucker beamed. "Right." He shook Sam's hand to confirm it.

Ben said, offhand, "We think that this lot might be worth about $5,000."

"We've asked Dave at the library to come over and have a look. Maybe he can help us identify some of the coins," Eadie added.

Tom and Liz looked at each other, bewildered. This situation was beyond their control. They were mere bystanders. Sam, Eadie, and Ben had done it all: read up on the history, figured out the probable location of the gold, and won over Mr. Tucker. It was all too incredible.

"And, Mr. Tucker," Eadie said, ignoring her parents, "I took a photograph of that silver spoon that we found at your place and I Googled it. I figured out the hallmark. It was made in London, England, in 1789. And the maker's mark, too. It was made by Hester Bateman. She was a famous lady silversmith. That spoon must be worth about $2,000 just by itself."

Mr. Tucker smiled at Eadie and shook his head in amazement. Sam high-fived him.

Liz picked up the phone and held it out to Ben. "Ben, call your parents and ask them to come over. They've got to hear this." She smiled. "I've got some pizzas in the freezer. You'll stay for supper, Mr. Tucker?"

Mr. Tucker beamed his pleasure.

Just then, Dave arrived on his bike and there were introductions all around. He was really glad to meet Mr. Tucker. He knew that Mr. Tucker was descended from one of the original pioneer families. And now he discovered that Mr. Tucker had the original copy of the Tucker land grant, Dave was hoping that he would lend this to the library for a history exhibit.

Supper was a lot of fun. Everyone was excited.

They all crowded around the kitchen table, eating pizza, with the pile of coins in the middle of the table. Across the room was the exposed wall of the log cabin, alias the shed-room. That log wall helped everyone to get their head around the reality of pioneer times on Commissioners Road.

Ben's parents were as astonished as Sam and Eadie's parents. They just couldn't believe how Sam, Eadie, and Ben had figured everything out. Ben's mum drew a sketch of Mr. Tucker, sitting in the kitchen, looking so happy, friends with everyone now. And Ben's dad was eager to see the shed-room and the log wall. He said that he would bring over an auger and figure out the years of growth in the logs.

Dave took a lot of photographs of the log wall. He was boggled. "If you guys ever need a history project for Mr. Grimshaw, you've got one in spades!"

And it was the first time that Mr. Tucker had eaten pizza! He was quite a picture sitting there with tomato sauce dribbling down his chin. He didn't seem like scary Old Tucker now.

Eadie showed everyone the pieces of broken pottery they'd found at Mr. Tucker's place. "I Googled it," she said. "Dymoke and Dymmick and, finally, Dymock. That's what it is — a village in Gloucestershire, England. That's where your family came from, isn't it, Mr. Tucker?"

"Yes, that's the story. I had heard it was Dimmock but didn't know where in England it was or how it to spell it. You're really quick on the computer, Eadie!"

Eadie smiled.

"I think I know what these pieces of pottery are," Ben's mum said. She turned to Mr. Tucker. "You say that your family first came here in 1809. I think that these pieces are from a special cup, a gift, that was made for the Tuckers by their friends in Dymock, to wish them well on their immigration to Canada. It would have been called a commemorative cup — to commemorate the occasion. See how big the letters are: bigger than would fit on an ordinary cup or mug. The cup would have been as big as a bowl and probably had two handles to lift it."

"It would have held a lot of beer!" Tom laughed.

Dave answered lots of questions about the coins. He explained that at the time of the War of 1812 there was very little coinage in the Canadian colonies because they were not allowed to mint their own coins. So all the English coins had to be sent out from London. And people used whatever coins they could get their hands on — even from different countries, like Spain and France. Anyway, it was so early in settlement that there were few families and few towns. Everyone grew their own food, and hunted and fished and money was not used much because there was nothing to buy. No shops. No services. No banks.

"When the war broke out, there was a real problem about buying supplies for the army," Dave explained. "There weren't enough coins circulating in Upper Canada to pay the soldiers and because of the war at sea it was risky to send shiploads of money out from England. So the military had the idea of printing Army Bills." He looked hard at Sam, Eadie, and Ben. "That was paper money, which the paymaster would have used instead of coins. He used it to buy food — flour, butter, meat, vegetables for the soldiers, and oats for the horses. The farmer or merchant could take the Army Bills to a government agent and it was treated like real money. So," Dave said, very slowly, "it will be remarkable if all these coins really were a paymaster's gold."

No one paid much attention to what Dave said. They were too excited by the shiny gold coins.

After supper, they set to work. Every coin was studied, turned over, discussed, and Googled for more information. Eadie photographed each coin, both sides. They tried to figure out the countries but many of the coins were in poor condition. They were so worn and the lettering so difficult to see that they couldn't Google them. They sorted those they could read by country: England, France, United States, Spain, Mexico, Portugal. Some weren't proper coins at all. Dave said that they were tokens issued by merchants, copying the idea of the Army Bills.

"Here's a token," Eadie said as she pulled it out of the pile."It just says 'Good for 5 cents in merchandise.' I wondered why it didn't have a country's name or king on it!"

They tried to get their minds around an early Upper Canada, lacking in towns and stores and banks. The merchants coping with all these different coins from different countries. But, with the help of the Internet and Dave, they started to understand how the system worked. They learned that sometimes the same coin had a different value. For example, if you lived in Upper Canada, you used a conversion scale called York currency, taking its name from New York. A Spanish dollar would be worth eight shillings York. But if you lived in the Maritimes, you used a scale called Halifax currency, which followed the system in Massachusetts. Then, a Spanish dollar would be worth five shillings. But in England, the Spanish dollar would be worth four shillings sixpence!

"I'd go crazy if I had a shop back then," Sam said. "How would you keep it all straight?"

But then Dave said, gently, "Well, let's sort the coins by date. See if it tells us anything more."

That's when they saw it.

It was so obvious.

Once they focused on dates rather than countries.

"Some of these coins have dates after 1814," Sam said, slowly.

"The latest one is 1848," Ben said.

"It's not our paymaster's gold," Eadie said, disappointed.

Everyone looked at the piles of coins on the table. They fell silent. How could this not be the paymaster's gold from the War of 1812?

Sam, Eadie, and Ben looked at each other. They couldn't believe it. After all the work they'd done — the research on the Web and in the library, figuring out the location of the old log cabin sites, hours out in the broiling sun with the metal detector, risking their lives with Mr. Tucker's dogs....

Dave broke the silence.

"That's history," he said. "Tricky stuff, history. You always know what you know. But you never know what you don't know."

Eadie looked at Sam and Ben. "Remember? We always said that we would find gold, somebody's gold, even if it wasn't General Procter's paymaster's gold."

"But we always thought, whatever gold we found, that it would be from the War of 1812." Sam got up from his chair and paced around the kitchen.

"Everyone used Commissioners Road, Sam," Tom said. "It was the main road for years after the War of 1812. This could be anyone's money. A later paymaster, a rich man's, a merchant's. Perhaps it was stolen and hidden by a thief."

Sam flung himself back in his chair. "I can't stand it! Not to know."

"But why was this money never found, for all this time?" Ben asked. "Whose was it? If a Tucker hid it, then it would have been claimed at some point, you would think. Who hid it, if it wasn't a Tucker?"

Mr. Tucker shook his head. He didn't know. There was no story in his family about hidden gold.

Eadie had been quiet while Sam raged. Now she spoke up. "So there's still a Legend of the Paymaster's Gold. We found gold, but we didn't solve the legend." She fingered the coins on the kitchen table.

Sam pushed his hair out of his eyes and calmed down a little. "We still get to keep the gold! And we know that it's worth a lot of money!"

Ben grinned and looked at both of them. "And the paymaster's gold is still there, somewhere, still waiting for us to find it."

"So, you'll be wanting to dig up my field again, eh?" Mr. Tucker said.

Everyone laughed.

"I was hoping that we would find that journal, or diary, or whatever it was that the scrap of paper was torn from. That John and Brad found in the shed-room," Eadie said. She looked at Dave and smiled. "But Dave says that a journal makes research too easy!"

Dave nodded. "It would've been easier if you'd found that journal, Eadie, but you guys did it your way. With phenomenal detective work."

"I've got an idea." Eadie sat up straight and looked around the table at everyone. "I'm going to write a story about this, as though I were fourteen and lived here, in our shed-room — although it would have been a log cabin then — on Commissioners Road, during the War of 1812. It would have been exciting. And frightening." She paused and turned to Mr. Tucker. "That silver spoon we found — the Hester Bateman marriage spoon — you said that there was an Annie Wareham who married into the Tuckers a long time ago? Her initials would fit in with those on the spoon. I'm going to call the girl in my story Annie Wareham."

Mr. Tucker beamed his approval.

February 1815

The war is over! I cannot believe it. Captain Rapelje rode by today to tell us the good news. I am not afraid anymore.

The next day, John arrived home! He walked all the way from the Niagara District. He is very thin, but very fit. We stayed up half the night hearing his adventures. Well, more frightening stories than adventures. He fought in many of the battles in the Niagara area: Stoney Creek and Beaver Dams and Chippewa and Lundy's Lane, which was the worst. And he limps now and he has a huge scar on his arm. And he has a sweetheart! She is called Nancy. He says that he is going to settle in the Niagara area to take on Nancy's father's place because both her brothers were killed in the war. That just makes me angry again — the killing, I mean — not Nancy. Lucy and I want to go to the wedding.

Thomas Greenaway's arm has not mended and William Greenaway has hurt his back. They are going to give up their land and try their luck in the town of York.

Father says now that John is going away for good, I will have to marry someone to get a strong young man on this farm to help with the work. Well, I will soon be seventeen! And now that the war is over, Lucy's father is writing to his brother in England to tell him to come to Canada. And he is to bring his four sons! Maybe one day I will marry a Tucker!

Author's Note

The War of 1812–1814 really happened. It happened in Upper Canada (Ontario) and Lower Canada (Quebec) and in the Maritime colonies (New Brunswick, Nova Scotia, Prince Edward Island, and Newfoundland). Commissioners Road, where Sam, Eadie, and Ben live, was there at the time of the War of 1812. In fact, it was a very important road in the small network of roads in the area. British soldiers and local militia used the road to travel between the Niagara and Detroit frontiers. Americans used the road to raid the Canadian settlers.

But Sam, Eadie, and Ben and their parents, as well as Dave and Mr. Tucker are made up by me. They live in the present day and are just trying to figure out what was going on in their neighbourhood during the War of 1812, because they have heard about the Legend of the Paymaster's Gold and want to find the missing gold. Annie Wareham, too, comes from my imagination, but she lived at the time of the War of 1812. Throughout the story, Sam and Eadie don't know that Annie lived in their shed-room (which was her log cabin) and watched the War of 1812 march by on Commissioners Road! She wrote about it in her journal, only a scrap of which was found.

I grew up on a farm very near Commissioners Road. We all knew about General Procter. He led some of the British soldiers during the War of 1812. And we all heard that story of how he might have lost some gold in a skirmish on Reservoir Hill. But no one has yet proved that the skirmish really happened, or whether gold really was lost. Captain Carroll and Captain Rapelje were real people in the local militias. Phoebe McNames was also a real person, recorded in various documents. Her gravestone is in the Brick Street Cemetery. But did the skirmish on Reservoir Hill really happen? If so, did Phoebe help the soldiers? You can Google all these names and find out more!

Reservoir Hill is there today, although a little changed from two hundred years ago! It has been widened and straightened to some extent, but if you go there, you can still see how steep and curving it was and how difficult it would have been for soldiers to climb up or down it on foot or horseback. Reservoir Park, at the top of the hill, contains the plaque that Sam and Eadie read. It tells of the American Andrew Westbrook and his raid against the Canadian settlers, and his being ambushed on the Reservoir Hill. It also tells of the death of Captain Carroll. I copied it exactly for this book.

It's exciting to think that there was a pioneer log cabin as part of Sam and Eadie's house. That is actually quite possible! I have seen such a case myself. The settlement conditions for applying for a grant of land, which Eadie learned from Dave in the library, are true. The settler had to build a cabin 16-by-20 feet, then clear 10 acres of land, a portion of the road, and trees for 100 feet back from the road. In such a way, the landscape was settled in an orderly pattern and the roads were built. It was clever of Eadie and Ben to see how they could use that information to figure out the location of former log cabins in today's landscape. And also to find the location of the original Tucker cabin (Lucy's home).

The fact that Eadie found two silver teaspoons at the site of the Tucker cabin is made up. But Hester Bateman isn't. She really was a silversmith in the eighteenth century. Her work is highly regarded today and is very valuable.

Coins were scarce in Upper Canada at the time of the War of 1812. There were few settlers, and there were few roads or towns to help the growth of stores and markets where money would be needed. The paymasters, who had to buy all the supplies that the soldiers needed usually paid the settlers with Army Bills just as Dave described. These were, in fact, paper promises, which were used as money. There were not yet any banks.

So, whose gold did Sam, Eadie, and Ben find? Perhaps it was a paymaster's gold, but from later than the War of 1812. Perhaps it was gold stolen from a settler by a thief who, for whatever reason, hid it or dropped it, and never came back to claim it. Sam, Eadie, and Ben don't know whose gold it was. But they did find it. And it is theirs. And Mr. Tucker's. Fifty-fifty.

ACKNOWLEDGEMENTS

I wish to acknowledge a number of perceptive readers, both youthful and adult, who contributed to the improvement of this manuscript: Joshua Bath, William Corfield, Kirsten McKay, Hilary Bates Neary, Jean Patey, Janet Rowe, Anna Shawyer, Susanne Shawyer, and Bruce Shawyer. I thank them for their encouragement.

Others helped to verify some points in my research: David Facey-Crowther and Ray Hobbs. Alberta Auringer Wood provided me with a stunning series of images of the military re-enactment of the Battle of Longwoods, 1814. Bruce Shawyer, as always, was a superb field assistant and technical advisor and best friend along the way.

I am grateful to Nicole Chaplin of Dundurn Press who cheerfully and skilfully guided me through the editorial process.

Some Books that Helped Me Write this Story

Glanville, Phillipa and Jennifer Faulds Goldsborough. *Women Silversmiths 1685–1845*. London: Thames and Hudson, 1990.

History of the County of Middlesex Canada. New Edition. Belleville: Mika Studio, 1972.

Illustrated Historical Atlas of the County of Middlesex. Reprint of 1878 edition. Toronto: Peter Martin Associates Limited, 1970.

Ontario Municipal Board. *Development Order 0166 Reservoir Park*. 2001.

Sheppard, George. *Plunder, Profit, and Paroles: A Social History of the War of 1812 in Upper Canada*. Montreal: McGill-Queen's University Press, 1994.

Shortt, Adam. *History of Canadian Currency and Banking 1600–1880*. Toronto: The Canadian Bankers' Association, 1986.

Shure, David. *Hester Bateman, Queen of English Silversmiths*. London: W.H. Allen, 1959.

St-Denis, Guy. *Byron: Pioneer Days in Westminster Township*. Frederick H. Armstrong, ed. Lambeth, London: Crinklaw Press, 1985.

Turner, Wesley B. *The War of 1812: The War that Both Sides Won*. Second Edition. Toronto: Dundurn Press, 2000.

WEBSITES OF INTEREST

http://www.chass.utoronto.ca/~banning/ANT%20 412/412coins.htm

http://faculty.marianopolis.edu/c.belanger/QuebecHistory/ encyclopedia

www.archives.gov.on.ca/English/exhibits/1812/index.html

www.warof1812.ca/

More Great Books for Young People

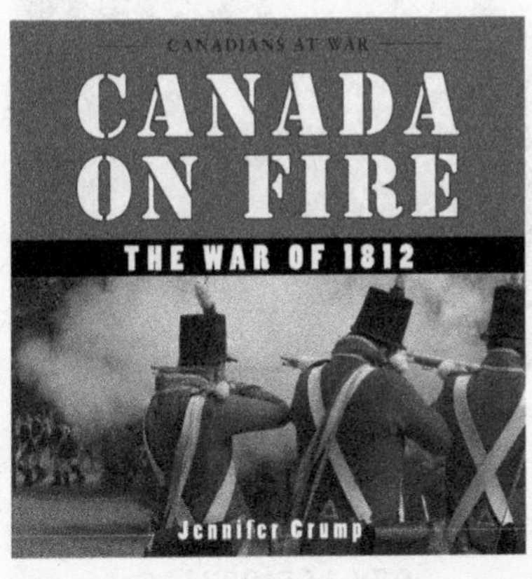

CANADA ON FIRE
The War of 1812
by Jennifer Crump
978-1554887538
$19.99

The summer of 1812 saw the beginning of one of the most brutal wars to take place on Canadian soil. *Canada on Fire* is an exciting account of the War of 1812 as told through the stories of the heroes who helped to defend Canada, people such as Mohawk chief John Norton, who led a small army into battle against the wishes of his tribe. With descriptions of the battle at Lundy's Lane, the adventures of the Sea Wolves, and the antics of James FitzGibbon and his Bloody Boys, *Canada on Fire* reveals the War of 1812 as it has seldom been seen.

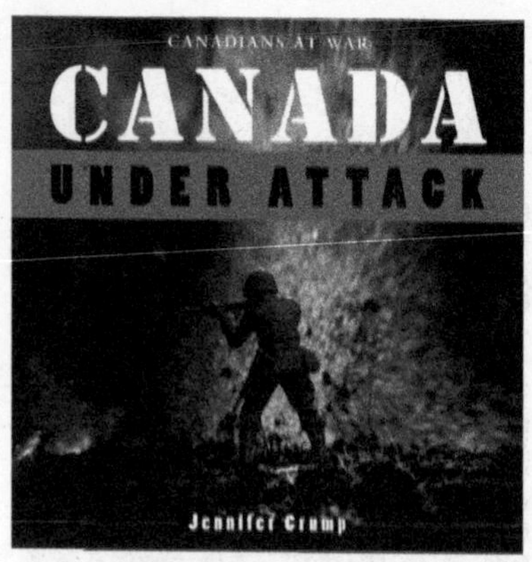

CANADA UNDER ATTACK
by Jennifer Crump
978-1554887316
$19.99

Most Canadians aren't aware that they've also had to defend themselves many times at home. Jennifer Crump brings to life the battles fought by Canadians to ensure the country's independence, from the almost ludicrous Pork n' Beans War to the deadly War of 1812 to the German U-boat battles in the Gulf of St. Lawrence in the Second World War. She reveals the complex American and German plans to invade and conquer Canada, including the nearly 100-page blueprint for invading Canada commissioned by the U.S. government in 1935 — a scheme that remains current today!

DUNDURN
www.dundurn.com